AMALGAMATION-1

'AN INSIGHT INTO THE LGBTQ+ COMMUNITY AND THEIR LITERATURE'

Editor: **Dr Pinki Chugh**

First Edition: Spring,2022

Spectrum Of Thoughts

AM/56, Basanti Colony, Rourkela, 769012, Odisha

An Affiliate Of FanatiXx

Website :- www.sotpublication.com

Published by Spectrum Of Thoughts 2022
Copyright © Pinki Chugh 2022
All Rights Reserved.

ISBN : 978-93-5452-534-6
Typesetted by: Mayuri Valanju
Cover Designed By: Sagar Samal

Disclaimer

This Anthology is an amalgamation of varied perspectives and experiences of study in literature. The writers have beautifully described their every emotion through their write-ups and they have given their words that the write-ups are free from plagiarism. They have given proper credits/citations with their writeups, for the sources they have used to research.

So, if any plagiarism is detected in the book neither the publishing house nor the editor will be responsible.

Foreword

'I am large, I contain multitudes.' (Walt Whitman)

Be it the Voice of God, or the whisper of the *Atma*; be it the cry of the stunted or the moan of the shamed; it prophetically proclaims the multifarious exhilaration as well as the exasperation of the human soul. Giving an ear to the unheard melodies is what Dr. Pinki Chugh commissioned to carry out in this book. An Amalgamation of different *Avathars* of the human soul with unique inner psyche is what she aspires to establish. Hence is this spiritual endeavour to make the good news known to the entire globe without painting in a moralistic hue.

Dr. Pinki, as the editor and compiler, has given a fine balance of perspectives towards this special psyche as chapters in which the issues related to the Lesbian, Gay, Bisexual, Transgender and Queer as members of the underrepresented spectrum of the rainbow, the pain and predicament of such souls in the journey of life, the need for a secured space and respectful recognition for decent living and a desperate cry for acceptance and accompaniment by fellow beings are dealt with. The well-defined eleven chapters, charted out of careful research and scrutiny exhibit a clear vision of championing the cause of the demeaned community. While the New Normal has become the watch word in the academic arena of the digital world and also in the familial system of the traditional ancient society of India, the anatomical, physiological and psychical difference too should be accepted as the New Normal. With this in mind researches have been carried out yielding fruit in the form of this book.

The first chapter of the book ***Art as a Protest: A Study of Laxmi's Autobiography Me Hijra… Me Laxmi!*** talks about the struggles of the protagonist for self-identification and talks about the ill-treatment of Hijras in the society. The chapter on ***History of Sexuality in Indian Culture*** criticizes the influences of moralistic canon of the

West on the much liberal East, especially the religiously and ethnically diverse culture of India and appreciates the scientific overtones attached to sexuality in Indian culture. Next chapter in the book, ***LGBTQ Characters in Fiction*** gives you an insight of all such LGBTQ+ Characters in different works of fiction from different authors belonging to different eras, right from the times of the origin of literature and homosexual terminology up to the modern times. The chapter on ***Challenges to Homosexuality: The Stereotypical View*** brings into limelight the challenges this rainbow community faces. Next chapter ***LGBTQ+ Couples' Challenges*** talks about the hardships of the same-sex couples and the societal prejudice they have to face in different ways. The trials and trivialities of the ***Gender Assessment*** by Society lead one ***to be or not to be*** who they are, according to their understanding as well as their urge. This has been the point of discussion in this chapter. ***Freedom for Nature-bound Roles in Shobha De's Selected Novels*** analyses how Shobha De's women characters do not have a strong need to acknowledge the ideological images imposed by patriarchal structure; rather, they want equal treatment in all spheres of life. ***Being LGBTQ In India: Some Home Truths*** sheds light on the difference in treatment of these belittled individuals in Urban and Provincial India. The chapter ***LGBT-Their History, Policies, Amendments and Literature*** discusses in detail the prevailing pathetic condition of the community in the modern era and shows how a new ray of hope is seen in their lives once the society strives for their inclusion. ***Transgenderism: a psycho-social facet of Dysphoria*** talks about the attempts being made by the scholars of various fields to re-establish and reassert the long-lost position of the queer community on the basis of both intellectual and cultural aspects of their identity. The chapter on ***Queer Theory: A Study on The Structure of The Autobiographical Texts*** pleads for exotification, acceptance and elevation not assassination of such community as they too are partners on earth.

Nowhere in the Hindu Itihas, or in the Christian Dogmas, or in the Islamic Tenets, or in any spiritual preaching were these psychic underpinnings condemned or rejected. It is high time during this accelerated change in social and family system, this group of brethren also must be given space to live with dignity because it is the true call they attend to, not anything that is an excessive selfish urge which harms the fellow being. This significant journey into the recesses of inner being of these is a much appreciated and welcomed endeavour towards a more humanitarian world in which machines are going to alternate human society.

It is a promising change to find the world's leaders of spirituality, morality and of letters, both young and old, enlightened to accept and accompany them to handle the varied sexual orientations of the diverse in Society. Dr. Pinki's edition and compilation is prophetically a clarion call to normalize interrelationship.

I wish God's blessings and graces go with you Dr. Pinki and your team of authors for your vision of creating a humanitarian society. May every reader find this book a blessing.

-Dr. Catherin Edward

Preface

Gender is not in anybody's hands. No one can choose his or her gender. It's as simple to understand as we have understood the chromosomes theory behind the child birth. In those days we fought with the evil of female foeticide and the governments came up with a law to ban gender testing before birth. Now our fight has taken up a new leap. Now again it is hard for even the so -called educated and aware section of the society to accept their children when they realise that they belong to the rainbow community. When general public does not agree to accept a simple law of nature, court of law has to intervene. Till the publication of this book, all eyes were on the court of law to grant equal rights to these sacred souls. Amendments in the article 377 of Indian Constitution were under discussion. Few revisions were made and few more were expected. But the implications were hard.

It becomes even harder when the victim is not ready to come out of the closet because of the fear being rejected.

This book is a small attempt to create a safer place for whole human kind without any prejudices. All the authors have put in their efforts to undertake substantial research to explore various facets of the issue.

The book will prove to be a great source for reference and citation in the further research /projects by the upcoming scholars.

Acknowledgement

Publishing an anthology is all about team work. My team comprised of so many cooperative intellectuals. Beginning with the biggest contributor, I sincerely offer my gratitude to Dr Catherin Edward.

Dr Catherin Edward has designed challenging yet appropriate and much needed curriculum for language teaching with ethics of life and profession, effective skills for communication and interpersonal relationships and lofty ideals for whole person development. She is the recipient of ***Bharat Shiksha Ratan Award by Global Society for Health and Educational Growth*** New Delhi, Sr Principal's Prize *for **Major Research Project*** from Holy Cross College and **Teachers' Research Grant**(TRG) by American Studies Centre Hyderabad twice between 1991 and 1994 along with **UGC Major Research Project Grant** 2009-2011 AIACHE Grant for **Research Assistance** in 1997.She has published various books and has contributed in various committees of experts (paper setter, research and curriculum designing).She has served on various dignified positions in the academia viz. Academic Council Member, Head of the department, Vice-Principal and Dean. She is the Convenor and President ELTAI Trichy Chapter 2018 till date. She has published research articles and served as Resource Person in International, National and Regional conferences. Her research output ranges from ELT, Material Production, American, African, African American, British, Canadian and Indian Literatures.

Very humble and decent person by heart, Madam Catherin had been generous enough to accept my request of writing a ***Foreword*** for this book, that too on a very short notice. Thank you so much madam.

Next in the list is **Dr Rashmi Gupta** who has made a very significant contribution to research. She is currently guiding Ph.D. research scholars from UTU as the Main Supervisor. She has published various research papers in national/international journals with high repute. She has published two books namely *"COVID 19: Pedagogical Issues,*

Challenges and Opportunities" and *"Psychological Impact of Pandemics in Different Eras."* She has her professional affiliation with "English Language Teachers Association of India." Apart from academics, she is the coordinator of Foreign Language Courses; Chief Editor of College Newsletter, College Prospectus and Convocation Brochure. Dr. Gupta had been honoured with Recognition Award 5 times. She has also received "Inspirational Woman Award 2020 for Best Performer in Education." Thank you so much madam.

I express my thanks to **Dr Renu Rani**, who is presently working as an Assistant Professor in the Department of Humanities & English Communication at College of Engineering, Roorkee. She has done her MA (English Literature), M.Phil (ELT) & Ph.D (Mythology) from Banasthali University, Rajasthan. Her areas of interest are interdisciplinary studies in Literature, Comparative Literature, Professional Communication and Adaptations.

I deeply acknowledge the contribution of **Dr Mukesh Kumar Gupta** who has always been a decent support in all the academic pursuits I ask for. He is currently working as an Assistant Professor in the Department of English, Govt. Degree College, Margubpur (Haridwar) affiliated to Sri Dev Suman Vishwavidyalaya, Tehri (Tehri Garhwal). He obtained his Ph.D. degree from Gurukul Kangri Vishwavidyalaya, Haridwar and PGCTE from English and Foreign Language University, Hyderabad. He has a number of research articles published in different national anthologies, journals and international journals.

I show gratitude to **Mr Animesh Sharma** who has also contributed a chapter. He is a marketing professional, a business man and an academician. He is a prolific writer, public speaker and a personality development mentor for budding professionals. Currently he is heading the department of English at KIHM, Dehradun.

Thanks a lot **Mr Rehansh Chaudhary** for being so quick and supporting me with other works besides contributing a chapter. Born and raised in the cultural town of Haridwar in North India, Rehansh

Chaudhary is passionate about his dreams and his creative imagination is the source for his stories. His priorities currently are set to the academics and spending time with his family and friends. If you won't find him doing all this, he'd be alone in a corner pinning down his thoughts on paper. Reading and writing are his hobbies. Not a researcher as such, he is a soulful writer by heart. Rehansh brought in light 'Zenobia' as his first book written in the tough times of the COVID pandemic. The friction shows a glimpse of a schoolboy's imagination. This book is available at

https://www.amazon.in/Zenobia-Twisted-School-Rehansh-Chaudhary-

I propose my heartfelt thanks to **Ms Nidhi Jindal** who is an Assistant Professor in College of Engineering Roorkee, Roorkee. She is an M.Phil , pursuing Ph.D from HNB Garhwal University. She spends most of her time in research writing. She has presented research papers in the area of English Literature and in International Conference by English Language Teachers Association of India. Her passion is to learn new things. She guides her UG students for research work and motivates them to dive into the ocean of creativity and innovation.

I also acknowledge the valuable involvement of **Ms Anamika Thapa**, Assistant Professor, School of Liberal Arts, Uttaranchal University, Dehradun for this book. She is pursuing her PhD in English Literature from Gurukul Kangri Vishwidhayala, Haridwar. She has a remarkable experience of teaching English Literature & Communication to UG students and 08 years of corporate experience. She is also a member of ELTAI, where she has attended several webinars and has also actively moderated various workshops, events and conferences.

Thank you so much **Ms S. Mariena Kamala Brinda Noel** for your contribution in the book. She is working as an Assistant Professor in English at Holy Cross College (Autonomous) Tiruchirappalli. Ms. Brinda is a passionate teacher and earnest learner and a psychologist.

She is an optimist. She believes in continuous learning and self-renewal. She loves teachings that empower and inspire people.

I cannot overlook the valuable contribution made by **Ms Srishti Upmanyu.** Srishti Upmanyu is an educator and an aspiring writer. She has written her master's dissertation and various chapters and articles throughout her academic and work life. Aspiring to become a screenwriter she has an interesting and varied flare of storytelling and narration based on her knowledge about India and the World. Thank you so much for working with me on this book.

I thank **Ms Anamika Saha** -a true literary enthusiast, for always being there at my beck and call during the process of compilation of this book. Anamika Saha is a PhD Scholar in Indian mythology and literature. Worked in Uttaranchal University as Assistant Professor in English, she enjoys scrutinizing every aspect around her that affects various art forms. Writing short poems and appreciating different art forms are favourites among her other interests. She has published papers in various journals and worked extensively on Ancient Indian philosophy and literature. She is associated with Doon Animal Welfare and tries to take care of all the deprived animals.

I offer my earnest thanks to **Ms Yashi Bansal** who is a post graduate in English Literature. She has work experience of more than 5 years in the field of teaching. She has worked as an Assistant Professor at Dev Bhoomi Uttarakhand University for more than 3 years. Ms. Bansal is the third author in a paper titled- *Machine Learning approach for identifying survival of Bone Marrow Transplant patients,* which was presented at ETCCS-2021 (Emerging Technologies for Computing, Communication and Smart Cities).

I express my solemn thankfulness to **Ms Anoushka Tyagi.** Anoushka is an avid content writer. She took Journalism & Mass communication as her subjects of study in graduation. Her aim is to use her knowledge of advertising, social media handling and content writing to secure an interesting career for herself. She writes blogs on positive and inspirational topics like *Pinning hopes for promising future, The sky starts* *breathing, Seeking help is not a stigma* etc. Apart from that, Anoushka is involved in event management also. She has worked as an executive member with a Wedding Planning Firm. She has also worked for *The Times of India* newspaper as a content provider under an internship program. She also works as a freelancer (content writing).

I enthusiastically thank the Heads of our team, Srashti Behure and Mayuri Valanju for their invaluable support in completing this mammoth project. I thank the **Spectrum of Thoughts**, **Fanatixx** team, for providing us such a creative platform.
Once again, I thank all the authors for their patience and faith in us, for co-operating, supporting and encouraging us at every step during the making of this Anthology.

I would like to give my unstinting thanks to the Designer, **Sagar Samal** for creating such an attractive cover page and the book's Interior Designers, Mayuri Valanju for lending their aesthetic expertise to the book.

Last but not the least we honour the blessings of the
almighty to have given us this opportunity to bring awareness in this society by contributing our bit.

-Pinki Chugh

INDEX

CHAPTER-1

Art as a Protest: A Study of Laxmi's Autobiography Me Hijra... Me Laxmi!

-Dr Mukesh Kumar Gupta
mkguptaghat@gmail.com

In the recent past, the literature dealing with the third gender has come to occupy a significant place in the world of literature and has attracted an interest that is wide spread. Laxmi Narayan Tripathi has carved an iconic niche for herself in the contemporary Indian scene, finding her literary inspiration in the sufferings and struggles of the third gender who are denied fundamental human and natural rights, even though they belong to the same species called Homo sapiens.

Her writing has been an impassioned tapestry of art and activism. Fired by anger at the injustice she sees around and tries to freeze the collective trauma of the people belonging to the fringes so that there will be something physical to remind the readers of the atrocities committed on a section of the society for ages. Her autobiography Me Hijra... Me Laxmi! is the voiced articulation of the third gender in contemporary Indian society. Her fiction transcends the bounds of literariness and can be considered as socially and politically committed, powerful statements in favour of the third gender. The author reveals his own dilemma regarding identity and existence and affirms everything by her passive word- 'We have to' or 'it's our fate'.

Laxmi does not stop merely with expressing her concern over the plight of the third gender but she goes beyond to explore and implant the seeds of protest and struggle through her art. Her memoir Me Hijra.. Me Laxmi! is recognised for giving voice to the voiceless. An effort is also made to explore amidst harrowing and depressing picture of Hijra community, springs flashes of human spirit for freedom, justice and beauty in her fiction.

There has always been an intimate connection between literature and life. Literature is said to anticipate life, copy it and mould it to its purpose. Literature like any other art form emerges not out of vacuum but out of concrete social reality at a given period of human history. Human life provides the raw material to which literature gives an artistic form. As Rene Wellek and Austin Warren put it: "Literature represents life; and life is in large measure a social reality ……." (94). It basically reflects the thoughts of its era and a writer presents the saga of a particular people or a community in the context of time against a certain background. As against the 'art for art's sake' theory a committed writer tries to re-create reality and at the same time tries to transform life through his work.

Laxmi uses this powerful instrument of art in form of writing to make her story circulate to whom she wants to transform into a sensitive and sensible agent for social change. Laxmi uses her sword of art and activism that is strong enough to strike and sharp enough to cut the very root of the evil. Through her art she shows that they (Hijras) refuse to live a clandestine life. They refuse to remain invisible and come to the public sphere to tell their stories. So, it is time for us to look at their productions and understand their engagement to overcome the layers of oppressions that exclude them from history.

Apart from Laxmi's Me Hijra... Me Laxmi! there are other books like The Truth About Me by A Revathi, A Gift of Goddess Lakshmi by Manobi Bandyopadhyay, and Red Lipstick: The Men in My Life by Laxmi Narayan Tripathi and Pooja Pandey come to Indian bookstores to challenge the logic of heteronormative system, which marginalizes gender identities that do not comply with the heterosexual, family, and reproductive model. They also tell their stories to denounce the dehumanizing living conditions of Hijras, with no rights as citizens. The Truth about Me: A Hijra Life Story (2010), Our Lives Our Words: Telling Aravani Life Stories (2012) and A Life in Trans activism (2016), Me Hijra … Me Laxmi! (2015) then Red Lipstick (2016) and

The Gift of Goddess Lakshmi (2017) are originally written in Tamil, Marathi and Bengali but translated into English, a language which provides greater visibility and international reach. This offers a possibility for the Hijras' situation to be known and discussed within and outside India. The translation into English contributes to the empowerment of the marginalized groups such as lesbian, gay, bisexual, transgender and other minorities.

Laxmi's writing functions as a counter discourse to all that is hegemonic, totalitarian and unitarian. It regards human beings as supreme and leads them toward total revolution. Thus, in marginal literature there is a paradigmatic shift from the grand narratives to the little narratives, from individual identity to group identity, from ideal to real, from self-justification to self-affirmation. For writers expressing concern for all those who toil and are exploited literature is not an expression of gaiety or celebration but a medium to voice the wounds of centuries of collective humiliation and exploitation, quest for selfhood, a revolution for social justice and an unprejudiced acceptance in society of the third gender. The chief endeavour is to create awareness amidst people of the grievances of the third gender.

The present paper analyses the plight of the third gender through the narrative art of Laxmi Narayan Tripathi in the form of protest. It explores the authentic side of the story of the Hijra Community and their social status. Laxmi remains loyal to her purpose of fighting for their rightful place in society, alongside herself. "I alone being respected wasn't enough. I wanted that respect to percolate down to the lowest of the low among the Hijras, so that we were all treated on par".

Laxmi occupies a unique position among marginal writers for her 'intellectual vigour'. She has made consistent use of myth and religion to convey the deep-rooted culture of Indian life and the origin of the Hijras. In the time of the Ramayana, Ram fought with demon Ravan and went to Sri Lanka to bring his wife, Sita, back to India. Before this, his father commanded Ram to leave Ayodhya (his native city) and go into the forest for 14 years. As he went, the whole city followed him because they loved him so. As Ram came to the banks of the river at the edge of the forest, he turned to the people and said, "Ladies and gents, please wipe your tears and go away". But those people who were not men or women did not know what to do. So, they stayed there because Ram did not ask them to go. They remained there 14 years and Ram returned from Lanka he found those people were there, all meditating. And so, they were blessed by Ram. It is believed that because of this blessing they have the power to bless the good fortune and fertility.

One origin myth of the Hijras is the story of Arjuna's exile. Vedic culture allowed transgender people of the third sex to live openly according to their gender identity and this is demonstrated in the Mahabharata story of Arjuna and Brihannala. Arjuna lives incognito for one year as a part of the price he must pay for losing a game of dice and also rejecting the advances of one of the celestial nymphs. Arjuna decides to hide himself in the guise of eunuch/transvestite, wearing bangles made of white conch, braiding his hair like a woman, clothing himself in female attire, and serving the ladies of the king's court (Rajagopalachari 1980). Some Hijras say that whoever is born on Arjuna's day, no matter where in the world, will become a Hijra. Another myth which is linked with eunuchs is tale of Mahabharata's Shikhandi. The story of Shikhandi in the epic tells us that Shikhandi had his rightful place in the society, although publically recognized as neither man, nor woman.

Mahabharata has a lot of characters and each character is related to the other by some or other way. The story of Aravan is one of the tragic stories of Mahabharata. Aravan was a fierce warrior. He fought bravely in the Kurukshetra war. Aravan sacrificed his life for the greater good. It is from his lineage that the transgenders are said to have been born. This is the reason why the transgenders are known as Aravanis. The transgender identity is celebrated in the Koovagam festival. Koothandavar temple is famous for its festival of transgenders and transvestites. Koovagam is a village in Ulundurpettai Taluk in Villupuram district of Tamil Nadu. Koothandavar temple is dedicated to the Lord Aravan/Koothandavar. The transgenders, who celebrate this festival, marry the Lord Aravan and become the brides for one day. This ritual is connected the myth of Mahabharata, when Aravan asked Lord Krishna for three boons. In his third boon, he asked Lord Krishna to be married before his death. But no woman was willing to marry for one day. So Lord Krishna took the avatar as "Mohini" and became the bride of Aravan for one day, and the next day Aravan sacrificed his life. In Koovagam festival after celebrating as the brides of Aravan for one day transgenders mourn Aravan's death by dancing and breaking their bangles. This festival is observed for eighteen days. It is a system of "hereditary stories which were once believed to be true by a particular cultural group, and which served to explain why the world is as it is and things happen as they do". In the Indian traditional family system these stories and myths have a unique importance as they pass it from generation to generation.

Having faced widespread discrimination and have human rights violated on a daily basis, Laxmi does not compromise with her situation but take decisions and protests through her art and activism. Despite question of class, caste, race, gender and patriarchy, she writes her own narration as an antidote to all form of discrimination. Laxmi's experiences and struggle; good and bad, profound and frivolous make strengthen Hijra community to protest. She does her duty as an activist, artist, celebrity, ambassador and phenomenal catalyst for change, for her community and for country.

She is first one Hizra who has overcome its fears for her identity, for her existence and start protest for the existence of Hijra community through her art. They are asserting that being transgender is an identity, not a disorder. By publicly assuming their gender identity, they are challenging the heteronormative discourses that have imprisoned them for ages for being the deviants (Foucault, 1988: 43). They are inscribing themselves in world history, showing how they apprehend everything that exists within the norms and beyond them.

Laxmi, despite being subjected to sexual abuse in her childhood and being discarded by society, she uses her art of dancing and writing not just for herself, but an entire community. "I discovered that passivity did not pay. It might endear me to society, but it came with a price. I decided at that moment to raise my voice against the things I did not like. Henceforth, I would not do anything against my will." She brings awareness about gender and sexuality and to discuss human rights democracy and equality in Indian society through her art. "What does it matter if you are a man, woman or hijra when something's got to be done? Why segregate yourself from mainstream society to such an extent?"

Laxmi stands up, fights for Hijra community and gets first chair of the Dai Welfare Society, she says, "I felt empowered, and empowerment is not a word that normally exists in the vocabulary of a Hijra. It is true that as a person, I, Laxmi Narayan Tripathi, liked taking on new challenges, but as a Hijra I was never allowed to." Later as activist she takes up new responsibilities with enthusiasm, she gives up dancing and devoted all her energies and intellect to bring about social change. She adds although she now is a full-time activist, it was dance that made her feel that she was also a part of mainstream society. Dance and activism, she says, are not much different from each other. "In both there is an expression of personal feelings and a message. Both dismantle the status quo," she writes in her book. But, when it came to choose between the two, she chose activism because it, "saved me when I was about to perish". On the other hand, when Laxmi is asked to leave the Bombay Gymkhana due to the 'no transgender persons allowed' rule, she demands an apology and doubles her efforts towards asking for a separate gender option for Hijras on government application forms. She declares, "Activism runs through my blood. It is the elixir of my life". Shaba Shabir says in his book review "Me Hijra, Me Laxmi serves as an educational narrative about the lives and paradigms of the Hijra community". Laxmi becomes the first transgender person to hold a passport in India and first transgender person to represent Asia Pacific at the United Nations for her community and India on several international platforms including speaking at the World AIDS conference on "Hijras and their problems", in Toronto. Even though every day back home is a fight for her, when Laxmi is granted diplomatic status to represent India at the UN in New York, she feels national pride: "I was no longer just Laxmi, the Hijra; I was India" even she also awarded 'Indian of the Year 2017'.

She also runs Astitva, an organisation for the support and development of sexual minorities. With a postgraduate degree in Bharatanatyam, Laxmi with her aim 'empowering the Hijra community' trains her troupe of Hijras and takes Amsterdam by storm by performing cultural dances at the Amsterdam India festival. Laxmi who starred in films, documentaries and TV shows such as 'Boogie Woogie', 'Between the Lines' 'Call it Slut', 'Bigg Boss' and 'Sach Ka Saamna' featuring Indian superstars Salman Khan and Sanjay Dutt, is called 'Laxmiji'. She shares, "the two of them, Salman and Sanjay, always referred to me as 'Laxmiji'. The suffix 'ji' is reserved for people worthy of respect. It has never been used for hijras".

Laxmi, agrees that several measures for the benefit of the third gender have been introduced by the government, but says that equal treatment of Hijras still remains far away in India. "I hope the government will devise a budget keeping in mind the third gender category or it might as well have someone represent us in the session," she says.

Regiane Correa De Oliveira Ramos in his article "The Voice of An Indian Trans Woman: A Hijra Biography" says, On April 15, 2014, in a landmark judgment, India's Supreme Court recognized transgender people as a third gender. Delivering the verdict, Justice K.S. Panicker Radhakrishnan asserted that "recognition of transgenders as a third gender is not a social or medical issue but a human rights issue" (Radhakrishnan, 2014). After two years of passing The Rights of Transgender Persons Bill, 2014 by parliament, Indian trans people are still fighting for their rights, and the Central and state governments have still not implemented some of the core directions given in the judgment, as pointed out by Vyjayanti Vasanta Mogli in an article in "The Wire"

Access to education and consequently to employment continue to evade the transgender community. Transpeople continue to face the violation of their right to life, facing unreported and unregistered hate crimes. There is very poor access to health and medical care, and many transpeople continue to be pathologised as having 'gender identity disorder' due to inaction by the Medical Council of India. (Mogli, 2016)

To make it more complicated, transsexuals, activists, academics and lawyers have questioned the definition of the term transgender in the "Transgender Persons (Protection of Rights) Bill, 2016".

The bill defines (i) "transgender person" as someone who is: (A) neither wholly female nor wholly male; or (B) a combination of female or male; or

(C) neither female nor male; and whose sense of gender does not match with the gender assigned to that person at the time of birth, and includes trans-men and transwomen, persons with intersex variations and gender-queers. (Transgender Persons Bill, 2016)

Sangama, an NGO for Sexual Minorities, and Reach Law filed a case for an amendment to be made in the definition, claiming that "Transgender Persons (Protection of Rights) Bill, 2016" completely distorts the historical legislation for transgender in India. For them, this definition is improper and derogatory, violating human rights, as it inhibits people from expressing their gender identity.

In September 2018 the Hon'ble Supreme Court of India made a ruling which was favourable to the LGBT community regarding section 377 of the IPC. In the context of that ruling, Laxmi established 'Kinnar Akhara'and participated in 2019 Kumbh Mela

However, we know that a law does not mean that the rights of transgender people will be respected. Also, a law does not guarantee that the mentality of people will be transformed overnight. In Me Hijra... Me Laxmi! Laxmi Narayan Tripathi registers her protest against the passive role of the Hijra community as a third gender. She advocates self-identification and condemns the treatment meted out to Hijras. Laxmi has been strikingly different from many contemporary novelists in the sense that She herself as protagonist is neither a super human being nor a helpless victim of patriarchal society. In the soul bearing autobiography Laxmi protests through her art of dancing, writing and activism to open an eye into the dark world of the Hijra.

Works-Cited

➢ Tripathi, Laxmi Narayan. Me Hijra... Me Laxmi! Trans. R. Raja Rao and P.G.Joshi. Oxford University Press. 2015. Print.

➢ Wellek, Rene and Austen Warren. Theory of Literature. 1949 (3rd Ed.). Harmondsworth: Penguin. 1968.

➢ Ramos, Regiane Correa De Oliveira. "The Voice of an Indian Trans Woman: A Hijra Autobiography" in Indialogs. Vol 5 2018, pp 71-88, ISSN: 2339-8523.

➢ Foucault, Michael. História da Sexualidade I: A Vontade de Saber. Rio de Janeiro: Graal. Mogli, Vyjayanti Vasanta. "Over Two Years After Landmark Judgment, Transgender People

➢ Are Still Struggling" in The Wire. <https://thewire.in/35978/over-two-years-after- landmark-judgment-transgender-peopleare-still-struggling/>

CHAPTER -2

History of Sexuality in Indian Culture

-Animesh Sharma
ex.animesh@gmail.com

The chapter attempts to cite facts about ancient India being one of the pioneer cultures to accept sexuality and acknowledge the presence of varied sexual orientations in a predominantly straight society. The essay would alongside highlight the facts that it was rather the West that brought about intolerance into an otherwise liberal East.

Introduction:

The seeming contradictions of Indian attitudes towards sex can be best explained through the context of history. India played a significant role in the history of sex, from writing the first literature that treated sexual intercourse as a science, to in modern times being the origin of the philosophical focus of new-age groups' attitudes on sex. It may be argued that India pioneered the use of sexual education through art and literature. As in all societies, there was a difference in sexual practices in India between common people and powerful rulers, with people in power often indulging in hedonistic lifestyles that were not representative of common moral attitudes. India is a multiethnic and multilingual society with wide variations in demographic situations and socioeconomic conditions. In a nation as religiously and ethnically diverse as India-the nation is commonly described as "a jumble of possibilities" -the people follow a wide variety of customs, and have varied beliefs that ultimately mold their lifestyles and sexuality. Sexuality means different things to different people. For some people, it could mean the act of sex and sexual practices, for others it could mean sexual orientation or identity and/or preference and yet for others it could mean desire and eroticism. Sexuality encompasses many ideas and has many facets. The definition of sexuality has been evolving along with our understanding of it. Sexuality is experienced and expressed in thoughts, fantasies, desires, beliefs, attitudes, values, behaviors, practices, roles and relationships. The first evidence of attitudes towards sex comes from the ancient texts of Hinduism, Buddhism and Jainism, the first of which are perhaps the oldest surviving literature in the world. These most ancient texts, the Vedas, reveal moral perspectives on sexuality, marriage and fertility prayers. It seems that polygamy was allowed during ancient times. In practice, this seems to have only been practiced by rulers, with common people maintaining a monogamous marriage. It is common in many cultures for a ruling class to practice both polyandry and polygamy as a way of preserving dynastic succession. Nudity in art was considered acceptable in southern India, as shown by the paintings at Ajanta and the sculptures of the time. It is likely that as in most countries with tropical climates, Indians from some regions did not need to wear clothes, and other than for fashion, there was no practical need to cover the upper half of the body. This is supported by historical evidence, which shows that men in many parts of ancient India mostly dressed only the lower half of their bodies with clothes and upper part of the body was covered by gold and precious stones, jewellery, while women used to wear traditional sarees made of silk and expensive clothes as a symbol of their wealth. Vatsyayana's classic work "Kamasutra" (Aphorisms of love) written somewhere between the 1st and 6th centuries includes the three pillars of the Hindu religion *"Dharma,"* *"Artha"* and *"Kama"* representing religious duty, worldly welfare and sensual aspects of life respectively. The main theme here appears to be the expression of Indian attitude toward sex as a central and natural component of Indian psyche and life.[1] The Panchatantra states that shyness, friendship, melodious voice, intellect, brilliance of youth, *enjoying the sensuality of women,* equanimity within the species, absence of sorrow/misery, *carnal pleasure,* religion, scriptures, intelligence of Brihaspathi (the teacher of Gods/Devathas), hygiene, concern about good behavior – *all these occur only when the creatures' stomach is full.* This elegant *Subhashitha* from Vishnusharma's Panchatantra clearly indicates the necessity of appropriate and adequate food/nutrition, a requisite for having the right mindset and power for optimum sexual performance. During 10th century to 12th century, some of India's most famous ancient works of art were produced, often freely depicting romantic themes and situations. Examples of this include the depiction of Apsaras, roughly equivalent to nymphs or sirens in European and Arabic mythology, on some ancient temples. The best and most famous example of this can be seen at the Khajuraho complex in central India built around 9th to 12th century. "The Perfumed Garden," by Sheikh Nafzawi, is the best known example of a classic Islamic sex manual. In this 16th century guide, what people of that time thought were the most satisfactory characteristics of lovers and love making, have been poetically and colorfully described.

Homosexuality Illustrations in Ancient India:

1. In the temples of Khajuraho, there are images of women erotically embracing other women and men displaying their genitals to each other. Scholars have generally explained this as an acknowledgement that people engaged in homosexual acts.
2. In the Valmiki Ramayana, Lord Rama's devotee and companion Hanuman is said to have seen Rakshasa women kissing and embracing other women.
3. At another place, the Ramayana tells the tale of a king named Dilip, who had two wives. He died without leaving a heir. The story says that Lord Shiva appeared in the dreams of the widowed queens and told them that if they made love to each other, they would have a child. The queens did as ordain by Lord Shiva and one of them got pregnant. They gave birth to a child, who went on to become famous king Bhagirath, best known for "having brought River Ganga from heaven to the earth".
4. The Mahabharata has an interesting story about Shikhandini, the feminine or transgender warrior of the time and responsible for the defeat and killing of Bhishma. Shikhandini was a daughter of King

Drupada, who raised her as a prince to take revenge from the Kurus, the rulers of Hastinapur. Drupada even got Shikhandini married to a woman. After her wife discovered the reality, she revolted. The day was saved by divine intervention bestowing Shikhandini with manhood during night. Shikhandini henceforth lived like a hermaphrodite.

5. During the great churning of milky ocean, according to Mastya Purana, Lord Vishnu took the form of a beautiful woman, Mohini to trick the demons so that the gods could drink all the amrut (the immortal juice found from churning of ocean). Meanwhile, Lord Shiva saw Vishnu as Mohini and instantly fell for him. Their union led to the birth of a child -- Lord Ayyappa.

6. Another scripture, the Narada Purana has references to what may be classified as "unnatural offences" described in Section 377. At one place, the Narada Purana states, anyone who discharges semen in non-vaginas, in those beings destitute of vulva, and uteruses of animals is a great sinner and will fall in hell. The purana does not approve of "unnatural offences" but the references prove that they were in practice.

7. The famous law code, Manusmriti provides for punishment to homosexual men and women. Manusmriti says that if a girl has sex with another girl, she is liable for a fine of two hundred coins and ten whiplashes. But if lesbian sex is performed by a mature woman on a girl, her head should be shaved or two of her fingers cut off as punishment. The woman should also be made to ride on a donkey.

8. In the case of homosexual males, Manusmriti says that sexual union between with two men brings loss of caste. If a man has sex with non-human females or with another man or indulges in anal or oral sex with women, he is liable for punishment as per the "Painful Heating Vow".

9. The ninth chapter of the Kamasutra of Vatsyayana -- composed in around 4th century BC, talks about oral sexual acts (Auparistaka), homosexuality and also of similar activities among transgenders (tritiya prakriti). The book, however, does not favour homosexuality of any kind.

10. Arthashastra of Kautilya -- a treatise on politics -- also mentions homosexuality. But the book makes it a duty of the king to punish those indulging in homosexuality and expects the ruler to fight against the "social evil".
Ancient Indian texts, inscriptions and paintings on temple walls, clearly, don't approve of homosexuality, but the repeated references do acknowledge its existence in those days.

Hence, it's evident that to uphold conformity to societal norms, unnatural sex was although reprimanded. However, it was acceptable as being an inherent part of society.

The Advent of Colonialism:

At the end of the medieval period in India and Europe, colonial powers such as the Portuguese, British and French were seeking ways of circumventing the Muslim controlled lands of western Asia, and re-opening ancient Greek and Roman trade routes with the fabled rich lands of India, resulting in the first attempts to sail around Africa, and circumnavigate the globe. The Indian Rebellion of 1857 caused widespread condemnation of the East India Company's alleged shortcomings and the Government of India Act 1858 completely did away with the Company's intermediary role, ushering in the British Raj era of direct rule. This put India much more at the mercy of Britain's official guardians of morality. Victorian values stigmatized Indian sexual liberalism. The pluralism of Hinduism, and its liberal attitudes were condemned as "barbaric" and proof of inferiority of the East. A number of movements were set up by prominent citizens, such as the Brahmo Samaj in Bengal and the Prarthana Samaj in Bombay Presidency, to work for the "reform" of Indian private and public life. Paradoxically, while this new consciousness led to the promotion of education for women and (eventually) a raise in the age of consent and reluctant acceptance of remarriage for widows, it also produced a puritanical attitude to sex even within marriage and the home.

Section 377, of the British colonial penal code criminalized all sexual acts "against the order of nature". The law was used to prosecute people engaging in oral and anal sex along with homosexual activity. The penal code remains in many former colonies and has been used to criminalize third gender people.

Homosexuality Illustrations in Modern India Writings:

There is widespread support for scrapping of Section 377 among writers and intellectuals in India and the likes of noted poet Vikram Seth and writer-politician Shashi Tharoor have openly advocated repealing of this Victorian-era statute. Amish Tripathi's arguments, however, are slightly different.

In his first non-fiction book Immortal India, Tripathi lays out the vast landscape of ancient Indian culture and argues that it had a fascinatingly modern outlook.

"I believe it's time we debated Section 377 of the Indian Penal Code that criminalizes sexual activity of LGBTs. It is an egregious and illiberal Section that must be repealed. There are some who have reservations based on cultural and religious grounds. Well, let's discuss them," Tripathi writes in his essay on LGBT rights before presenting his arguments, validated by his research and knowledge of Hindu mythology.

"I am not an expert on religious mythologies of other religions, but as far as Hindu scriptures are concerned, I think there are ample examples to substantiate that LGBT rights were accepted in ancient India," Tripathi told IANS when asked what made him reach this conclusion.

His essay in the book is written from a Hindu perspective and draws immensely from ancient scriptures. He cites several examples and anecdotes from Hindu religious texts to make his point – that LGBT rights were accepted in ancient India.

"Purush napunsak nari va jiv charachar koi / Sarv bhav bhaj kapat taji mohi param priy soi. (Any man, any transgender, any woman, any living being, as long as they give up deceit and come to me with love for all, they are dearest to me.)"

"These lines were said by Lord Ram in the Ramcharitmanas. He did not differentiate between man, woman or transgender. What does this mean? According to me, this shows our liberal ancient attitude towards LGBTs. And there are other examples in the Mahabharata too. Such stories were celebrated in ancient India and this, to my mind, reflects the liberal attitude we had towards LGBT communities," he elaborated.

Tripathi also argues in the book that Section 377 does not reflect the traditional Indian attitude towards sex. It is, instead, he argues, a reflection of the British colonial mindset, influenced by medieval interpretations of Christianity.

"I think there is a great deal to learn from such examples. If we had such a society, which accepted LGBT communities with openness in ancient India, I surely think we can think on similar lines today as well. Also, on the principle of individual liberty, if heterosexuals can lead their lives in the way that they see fit, then LGBT communities should also have the same rights and freedoms to decide how they want to lead their lives," he maintained.

The best-selling author with gross retail sales of over Rs 100 crore further asserted that religion is an integral part of most societies but, in his opinion, modern laws should be based on individual liberty rather than on any religion.

"I am a very proud Hindu and I am a very religious person, but I do not think that religious beliefs should lay the foundation of any laws in the modern world. Modern laws should be based on the concept of individual rights and liberty. Everybody should enjoy equal freedom and rights in all aspects. Religion has a very important place in society. But laws should be based on secular principles and individual liberty, and they should not be influenced by any religion," he contended.

Tripathi's mythological fiction titles have sold more than four million copies and have been translated into about 20 languages. He worked for 14 years in the financial services industry and quit it only after, in his own words, his royalty check became greater than his salary.

In many former colonies it has been repealed or is no longer enforceable. In India too, on 24 August 2017, India's Supreme Court gave the country's LGBT community the freedom to safely express their sexual orientation. Therefore, an individual's sexual orientation is protected under the country's Right to Privacy law.

References:

1. https://journals.sagepub.com/doi/full/10.1177/2631831818822017
2. https://www.tandfonline.com/doi/pdf/10.1080/02674659408409567
3. https://timesofindia.indiatimes.com/life-style/relationships/love-sex/40-of-indian-wives-have-regular-sexual-intercourse-with-men-other-than-her-husband-report/articleshow/74320414.cmshttps://www.ncbi.nlm.nih.gov/pmc/articles/PMC3705691/
4. https://www.goodreads.com/work/quotes/70913254-ram-chandra-series-book-1-and-book-2

CHAPTER-3

LGBTQ Characters in Fiction

-Anamika Thapa
anamikathapa88@gmail.com

Fiction often considered as the broadest category of literature is mainly composed of the writer's imagination. It has no boundations and no limits, probably that's the reason it is the most liked genre when it comes to literature. But it is not necessary that everything included in fiction is imaginative, it also deals with the people, things and emotions that are a part of our daily lives and the society. And one such part of the society that we live in is the LGBTQ community. Have you ever come across the LGBTQ characters in any kind of fiction (romance, horror, science, etc.)? If not so, the following paragraphs are for you to get familiar with these common but special characters without which the stories would be nothing but mediocre piece of scribbling and boring.

There are a lot of characters in fiction who belong to the LGBTQ Community but most of the readers might not be aware of it until now, for instance, Albus Dumbledore from the best-selling series of its times, *Harry Potter*. Few people know about the sexual identity of this beloved character. Similarly, most of the times we, as readers, neglect any such hints about the homosexuality of any characters in various works of fiction. Hence, here this chapter gives you an insight of all such LGBTQ+ Characters in different works of fiction from different authors belonging to different eras, right from the times of the origin of literature and homosexual terminology up to the modern times. It not only gives you an overview of these characters but also explains their significance in the story and how we ended up in the conclusion of their sexual identity being homosexual and not heterosexual.

Gore Vidal once said, ***"The important thing is not the object of love but the emotion itself."*** And this statement, somewhere forces us all to spare a thought about the LGBTQ community. When this word 'LOVE' pops up, it is usually considered to be a romantic relationship between two different sexes. People having love interest in the same sex are looked down by the society even now. As per the societal norms, they are mostly forbidden from various social activities as well.

For such people who are either interested in the people of same sex, or both and those who belong to the third gender, a specific term, 'LGBT' has been derived. It stands for Lesbian, Gay, Bisexual and Transgender. With advancement in various technological and philosophical domains, we now live in a world where people are quite open – minded and accept the changes around us open arms. We now consider equality to be an integral part of any association. But continuing to be sexiest, and with LGBT community still being underrated does not align with basic human rights and endangers the progress of our generation. We need to work towards equality at all possible levels.

With all the oppression and backlash that this community had faced in the past few years, or is still facing to some extent, the time now demands us to not sit as mute spectators. So, let us put our sleeves up and learn that this world will have to put up with our so called 'annoying' behaviour.

Considering all these frivolities faced by the LGBTQ community, many people have extended their support to them through various means. Considerate people are helping them out to fight the odds of the society in their best way possible. And one such help is done by various writers by including LGBTQ+ characters in their works of fiction to encourage these people fighting for their rights.

The letter Q in LGBTQ is basically a popular variant used for those who are identified as queer or are still questioning their sexual or gender identity. Since, in today's world, with keen readers spread across the globe, the writings do have a long-lasting impact on the minds of people. What the audience (either targeted one or the non-targeted) reads in any book, magazine, or journal they do give a thought to the agenda of the topic and consider it to be quite an integral part of our daily lives. So, the basic idea of including LGBTQ+ characters in the works of fiction are to build up a mindset of the people that if someone belongs to this community, he/she is not a sinner and we as responsible citizens should avoid abandoning them and making them feel left out.

The historical concept and definition of an individual's sexual interest have been changed over the time. For instance, the term 'gay' was not used to describe someone's sexual orientation until the mid of 20th century. But in recent times, it has become a widely used term whereas now in the United States of America, the word, homosexual, seems to receive some negative feedback from the people. And soon with the changing times, people belonging to the bisexual and transgender community also made up their space and got recognition in the larger minority community i.e., the LGBTQ+ community.

However, during the initial days the people belonging to the transgender and gay community suffered massive backlash by the critics. They considered the bisexual people to be either gay men or lesbian women who fear revealing their identity to the common masses and, they said the transgender to be breaking the stereotypes of the society we live in. But after years of fighting against all odds, these people have made up space in the society and are also appreciated in various works of fiction. There are instances of gay characters breaking barriers in different genres.

When talking about the LGBTQ characters in fiction, it can be of any genre, for example, science fiction, historical fiction, mythological fiction, fantasy, romance, horror and can be in any form such as in writings (in the form of stories and poems or songs), movies, television dramas, theatre, etc. When it comes to literature, it can be categorized into different domains like the gay literature, the lesbian literature, history of bisexual and transgender community and history of their origin and so on.

Throwing light upon the lesbian literature, it basically comprises of poetry, plays, writings and fiction that addresses the lesbian characters and non – fiction that addresses the topics related to lesbian interests. This literature includes the works by lesbian authors, irrespective of the genre and extract of their work, as well as those works of heterosexual authors which are lesbian – themed. The fundamental work of lesbian literature is the poetry of **"Sappho of Lesbos."**

Sappho was an Archaic Greek poet born in 630 B.C. in the island of Lesbos and died in 570 B.C. She is still well known for her lyric poetry, which is written to be sung along with the music. She still manages to be the source of inspiration to many modern aspiring writers or poets when it comes to extraordinary poetry techniques. Her poetry depicts her love for women who are clearly expressed in her various works. Beyond the poetry, she is also considered as a symbol of love and desire between women. The English words 'Sapphic' and 'lesbian' are also derived from her name and the name of her home island, which clearly demonstrates that she has played a significant role in the upliftment of the lesbian community and has contributed a lot to the lesbian literature through her poetry.

Now let us investigate the Gay Literature, Like the lesbian literature that has been discussed earlier, gay literature is also a collective term composed of the literature that is either written by gay authors or the works of heterosexual authors that has gay themes in it, which may include the plot lines, the characters or the themes that support the male homosexual behavior. Gay literature is also inspired by the stories of romantic affection or sexuality between men in the ancient and classical mythology. Though these stories are just mere myths, but they are still considered as the forms of LGBTQ expression and the modern concepts of gender and sexuality are considered in this regard.

Apart from the lesbian literature and the gay literature, homosexuality is also referred in the speculative fiction as the incorporation of the different homosexual themes into fantasy, horror fiction, science fiction and many other related genres. In such works of fiction, the main elements may include a lesbian, gay, bisexual or transgender (LGBT) characters as the protagonist or such characters may contribute to the major plot or climax of the story or drama.

A few decades ago, people or more specifically the authors were not confident enough to express their thoughts frankly about the third gender or the lesbian and gay communities in their writings. They were even hesitant to include characters from the LGBTQ community in their works of fiction. But with the time, today, writers have much more freedom with their style of writing and their content. Earlier if they had to talk about any sexual orientation or identity other than the heterosexual one so they would simply hint at it, but now, they have the liberty to merely term such characters as lesbian, gay, bisexual, or transgender characters or simply state that they belong to the LGBT community.

There are way too many examples for the same, where the characters belong to the LGBTQ community in the works of fiction. Let us investigate such characters - The first work is **The Vampire Chronicles** by Ann Rice, it is a series of novels and media franchise. The story revolves around the character **Lest at de Lion court**, the 1976 character who is basically a French nobleman who later turned into a vampire in the 18th century. His autobiography is written in the second novel of this series and his sexual identity is hence developed to be bisexual who has both male and female love interests as both a vampire and a mortal. He actually gets more inclined towards that person whosoever most interests him at a particular point of time. This character struggles with the questions of his existence in the universe and is philanthropic in nature. Few such references from the book which describes the LGBTQ character of Lest at de Lion court is as follows:"...*We were at that moment of drunkenness that the two of us had come to call the Golden Moment, when everything made sense. We always*

tried to stretch out that moment, and then inevitably one of us would confess,"
I can't follow anymore, I think the Golden Moment's passed..."

"...I was still sitting there, too unsure of myself to say anything, when Nicolas
kissed me.

'Let's go to bed,' he said softly."

The next work is by the famous author of his times, Oscar Wilde, the philosophical novel by him titled as **The Picture of Dorian Gray.** Here, the main character, **Dorian Gray** shows certain characteristics of being homosexual in nature. This novel was written by Wilde in the early 1890s. Also, this novel consisting of certain overtones of homosexual feelings was banned back then, stating the reason to be its sexual undertones. As during that period, people would not accept the LGBTQ characteristics in the characters so easily or openly and that too in the main character of the story. One such line of Dorian Gray from the book which puts confirmation on his gay identity is -

"It is quite true I have worshipped you with far more romance of feeling than a man should ever give to a friend. Somehow, I have never loved a woman...From the moment I met you, your personality had the most extraordinary influence over me...I adored you madly, extravagantly, absurdly. I was jealous of everyone to whom you spoke. I wanted you all to myself. I was only happy when I was with you."

Scott Pilgrim graphic story series by the Canadian author, Bryan Lee O' Malley, which is a comic series of six novels. The series revolves around the story of a slacker and a part – time musician, Scott Pilgrim, whose quest is to vanquish his dream girl's seven ex – boyfriends. His friend and roommate, whom he met in the college, **Wallace Walls,** acts as his voice of reason in his journey. Hence, this character, Wallace Walls, tends to show some homosexual characteristics, since they both share a double bed as they cannot afford two separate beds. And, there are several instances throughout the story where readers can find out Wallace Walls showing sexual interest in Scott Pilgrim, hence, confirming the gay identity of his character. But apart from

Wallace's gay character, there are many other LGBTQ references in the books by Scott Pilgrim as well, some of his such line are -"*...because I'm in lesbians with you. I really, really mean it.*"

"Anyway, how are you and Ramona doing?'

Uh... you know. Pretty good.'

Have you said the L-word yet?'

The L-word? You mean? Lesbian?'

Uh... No. The other L-word.'

?'

Okay. Uh, It's "love." I wasn't trying to trick you or anything..."

The other is the character of **Lisbeth Salander** from **The Girl with the Dragon Tattoo**, written by the Swedish author and journalist, Steig Larsson. Here, the lead fictional character, Lisbeth Salander, has a bisexual identity who took down the culture of instutionalized rape in the world of literature and it is to some extent due to the ambiguity of her sexual identity that readers of different age groups and different sexes found this trilogy quite fascinating. Even most of the feminists also considered the character of Lisbeth Salander to be third – waver. In the story its quite obvious that she has bisexual relationships with her different friends and emotionless coolness. By the end of the first book, this character could be considered as a smart and independent woman who is sexually aggressive, physically fearless, indomitable and the one who becomes very rich. Here a few lines from the book which hints at the gender ambiguity of Salander -

"...What do you need me for?

Salander's greatest fear, which was so huge and so black that it was of phobic proportions, was that people would laugh at her feelings. And all of a sudden all her carefully constructed self – confidence seemed to crumble."

Harry Potter by J.K. Rowling. Harry Potter is an emotion, with its resounding success and crazy fan following, a lot of people might already be aware of the homosexual character in this world-famous franchise. Yes, you guessed it right, it' none other than one of the prominent characters of the series, **Albus Dumbledore.** Although the sexual identity of Dumbledore has never been specified in any of the books of the series but some fans wondered if he was a gay as there is also no mention of his love interest and children in the books. And, putting halt to all these confusions, the author herself clarified that Dumbledore is a gay. During an interactive session with the audience in 2007 one of the students asked the author about the sexual identity of Albus Dumbledore, to which she replied, "My truthful answer to you... I always thought of Dumbledore as gay."

Talking about whom Dumbledore fell in love with, it is believed that it was none other than the bad wizard whom he defeated long ago, **Gellert Grindelwald.** Dumbledore met Grindelwald in the summer before he graduated from Hogwarts, just after the death of his mother, but later this love interest added to his horror when Grindelwald showed him his true colors (his evil side). The author, about Dumbledore and Grindelwald, even once stated, "Their relationship was incredibly intense, it was passionate and it was a love relationship."

The next homosexual characters in the fictional world are **Ennis Del Mar** and **Jack Twist** from the short story **Brokeback Mountain** written by the American author Annie Proulx. Ennis and Jack were two shepherds during the 1960s who tend to develop sexual and emotional relationship with each other but must keep it a secret since, during those times gay men were beaten to death in Wyoming, where they were residing, as homosexual relationships were not acceptable at that period in major parts of the society. Also, later their relationship becomes even more complicated when both were married to their respective girlfriends. There is a famous line by Jack Twist in the play which he says to Ennis Del Mar, which puts a confirmation to their sexuality as a gay, and that line by Jack is -

"I wish I knew how to quit you."

Also, as the time passes by and the two men grow older, they use to hardly meet each other but their fondness and longing to see each other never diminished. While, Ennis managed to bury his feelings as deep as he can, on the other hand, Jack was not able to hold them up any more and was so desperate for both of them to be together and tells the audience that how badly he misses Ennis -

"...Sometimes I miss you so much, I can hardly stand it..."

This list of homosexual or LGBTQ+ characters in fiction is never ending because in certain instances in almost every fictional work there is a hint of homosexuality of a particular character. To all intents and purposes, these characters undoubtedly play a significant role in the plot and for the advancement of the story. Now, with changing times people accept the homosexuality of the characters in a positive way without any massive criticism. This not only boosts up the confidence of writers to include homosexuality in their works but also is a major turning point in the survival history of the LGBTQ community.

But including certain LGBTQ+ characters in their work, does it make that particular book LGBTQ? Well, not necessarily. For a book or novel to be considered as a LGBTQ book, firstly, the main character of that story should either belon to the LGBTQ Community or he/she should have some clearly mentioned or defined LGBTQ issue in their characterization. Second thing which is important is that along with the main character, the centre of the plot of the story should also be based on either the homosexuality concept or the LGBTQ issues. Hence, it is not necessary that if there are LGBTQ characters in a work of fiction so the whole book is based on it, sometimes such elements or characters are a part of the story just to make it more intriguing for the readers or for adding some issues touch to the plot of the story.

Hope this article was able to answer all you question about the LGBTQ characters in certain works of fiction and now you have an insight of their importance in the story and by what references were these characters considered to be belonging to the LGBTQ community.

References:

1. The Picture of Dorian Gray by Oscar Wilde ISBN-10 9789380005478 ISBN-13- 978-9380005478, Publisher-Maple Press, Publication date - 1 September 2013

2. https://www.123helpme.com/essay/Homosexual-Elements-in-The-Picture-of-Dorian-12222

3. https://www.researchgate.net/publication/292473067_The_Gender_Ambiguity_of_Lisbeth_Salander_Third-Wave_Feminist_Hero

4. The Girl with the Dragon Tattoo Book 1 (Millennium Trilogy), Publisher- RHUS, Publication date- Publication date-13 November 2012, ISBN-10 - 1401235573 , ISBN-13 - ISBN-13-978-1401235574

5. Harry Potter Box Book Set: The Complete Series (Set of 7 Books) [Paperback, English], ASIN : B09P5CGKL1

6. Brokeback Mountain, Publisher – HarperCollins, Publication date - 3 March 2006, ISBN-10 – 0007240031, ISBN-13 - 978-0007240036

7. https://writersrelief.com/2015/06/17/beloved-lgbt-literary-characters/

CHAPTER -4

Challenges to Homosexuality: The Stereotypical View

-Rehansh Chaudhary
fmail8554@gmail.com

"It's just a phase."
"You can control this!"
"You're better than this."
"This is WRONG."

Can we really control who or what we are attracted to? Can you? At least that is what people expect from the whole community indulging into same-sex relationships. Treating them as inhumane or threating their existence in ways one can only imagine. You think I'm exaggerating? Read along then as here I try to give something people usually are interested in- 'a reality check', as I shed some light on the confusing yet important issue of stereotyping against the LGBT+ people. Hotheads tend to form some maniacal opinions about the things they do not understand, just to suit their own thinking, feeding the world with stereotypes or clichés or theories that are no way true. The concept of LGBT is one such issue, still there are innumerable individuals who aren't aware about this and many out there who interpret this as wrong, resulting in stereotyping.

Everyone has the right to live their life in any possible way they want to and if someone, in this case, LGBT+ member tries to follow unconventionalities, people give them shit! Everyone has right to 'form' opinions, nobody's stopping you from doing that but if you think you are supreme enough to 'impose' these vague thoughts on others and make them follow you, you are so not right! Stereotypes, are nothing but generalizations formulated into basic beliefs which go on to become culturally accepted. There is a fine line between truth and stereotypes but many of us out there just overshadow the line, not bothering to confirm what's true and what is not- just barging in the society spreading word about the misconceptions.

Numbers don't lie, at least that is what the data figures over the last six years represent. Discrimination still prevails in all fields, but it prevails more in the LGBT community front than the "straight" clan. The survey reports of 2016 shows that one in every four LGBT persons face discrimination and are stereotyped. These figures in the changing years have fluctuated but the average still remains the same. This study is one of the ample pieces of evidence which proves the ongoing vendetta against gay community by a large part of our society. All this starts from homophobia, which is the fear of being perceived as gay which causes social disapproval and discrimination against LGBT. Being tagged as different or even worse, wrong, is something which ignites the hate crimes. This chain leading to difficulties for gay men has a root cause- 'the stereotypes.' When we already imagine the worst about them, and consider it true thereby starting to hate them- which leads to getting converted into homophobes making the lives of LGBT+ miserable.

The feminine guys: Gays! Forgive me for disappointing all the people who think this is true, allow me to present this reality check to you; thinking that femininity and gayness are interrelated is just a glimpse of our perceptive view about gay-guys. The idea that being a lesbian means being a masculine lady or being gay meaning feminine men is untrue on all grounds. This view is so strongly believed that the challenges made against the statement are of no use. While the fact that there are feminine gay men is true but the other part stating masculine men can be gay holds as much truth as the other one. There are many instances of masculine men coming out and speaking about their true identity. The same applies for masculinity and lesbian women. Masculine women may be straight or they may be gay which itself speaks that; lesbians always aren't masculine. These are two separate notions and when combined create confusion and false intel in people's mind, leading to several other interconnected clichés. For instances, sports are anti-gay! I'm pretty sure many of you believe this.

Haven't you heard of even one sportsperson announcing their sexual orientation? Haven't you heard of gay guys liking sports? Or let's tackle a different route, don't you have any straight guy friend who's into ballet or any other so called 'girly' activities? People just tend to find the answers to everything even when things are not meant to explained but just stated as factual statements. Here's the thing, why are you gay? Is not a valid question or maybe it is? Either way, it has got nothing to do with the subject of your masculinity or femininity or are you into sports or not, it's about who you are attracted to or who do you prefer. So, stop putting a tag cause it's not up for debate.

"Look at the way you dress, you can never be gay!"

"Why are you so gay? It's just something about the way you dress, I think."

Have you ever seen somebody buy clothes as, show me the dresses for gay men, I'm straight-show me the clothes? I'll make it easier for you, you haven't. Not because you haven't encountered enough LGBT people but because the way you dress does not define your sexuality and neither does the way you speak. These are just a couple of the numerous misconceptions people have about the community. LGBT+ individuals are expected to walk, talk, dress and behave in a certain manner with the slurs like 'how can you be gay' or 'why are you so gay' making it hard on them. Every dress is open to every *Homo sapiens*, man or woman. You can wear a tank top and be a straight guy or wear baggy clothes be "looking like a man" and still be a woman, because who are we kidding; these things are much more comfortable as compared to our regular clothing.

"All gay men are sexual predators or pedophiles." No, they aren't. they are simply males who happen to be sexually attracted to or like other men. The UC Davis researchers point out, gay men and women only account for less than one percent of all molestation cases in which an adult was identified. How does that sound? The idea that gay men possess a grave danger to the world because of their tendency of sexual predation is a meek theory based on a few cases out of the literally infinite instances.

"It will eventually pass." Will it though? Being queer is not a phase. It is an identification. If you want to believe it, that is your choice but I'd like to take this time to falsify these claims or allegations or just baseless comments and say that being gay is reality. People who are gay do not switch from straight to gay month to month because it's fun. Maybe it is confusing and figuring it out may take some time and it is a possibility that one or more may consider it a phase, but it does not mean that this is something which will go away eventually.

Do you have a religion? Well, your answer to that question might be, "Doesn't everyone?" Yes, everyone has a religion and everybody is somehow connected to spirituality. Then why does parts of our society think that gay people have rejected religion or they have been kicked out of it? Or LGBT+ have given up on spirituality? "You can't be queer and religious." Is just a baseless notion. Though in many religions, homosexuality is considered a sin but that does not mean that one stops practicing his/her religion only because they're gay. What your sexuality is and how you worship are two entirely different concepts, for instance who do you want to have sex with is not followed by who do you worship? Intermixing the two just doesn't make any sense. The bottom line is you may be the religious or not- it has got nothing to do with how you identify yourself.

These are just a handful of wrongly perceived thought about LGBT community. There are several others which leads up to many undignified hate crimes against them. But not just that, the discrimination starts from the ground zero at every place including workplace offices, schools and society at large. Even small incidents of hate may affect the life of someone in a destructive way, be it a closeted member or out and about person from the LGBT community.

Children tease each other in ways that no human adult can imagine, that right there, is ground level zero. Suppose there is a closeted gay friend playing with his friends when someone is given a friendly tease about their heterosexuality, the closeted one tend to develop a fear of identity and acceptance from that early stage. Challenging someone's heterosexuality at every point or using "gay" as insult is not cool! This causes trauma causing delayed coming out or sense of permanent fear based on the expectations of rejection from family and social life.

Workplace should ensure a psychologically and physically safe space for everyone. But what if it does not feel like a safe place or even worse, what if your whole existence is questioned there? This is close to what many of the LGBT+ members undergo and experience. This ranges from all sorts of discriminative behaviors; getting treated as a woman if you're gay, denied promotions or even getting fired just because of how one identifies themselves. This brings into play the minority stress theory which becomes more prominent if you're a person of color on top of being gay, this causes internal trauma forcing LGBT people to adapt to things they do not want to such as dressing up their voices or wearing certain colors to work or ensuring no slipup in any aspect of their job. Other than jobs: choosing the 'right' store to buy groceries or 'appropriate' transport make gay people cave. This is not just the case with workplaces but also schools, colleges, neighborhood, spiritual institutions where the discrimination does not let you "fit in."

Many notions are likely to take up a form which leads to the world seeing LGBT in a completely different manner. Like thinking all transgender women are drag queens or that asexual people have no libido, or that all lesbians hate men; these are screwed up opinions shaping public view.

The stereotypical views take up lager forms when they come into play as discriminations leading to more dangerous forms of violence and harassment. It is not just about the stereotypes then; it takes a violent turn. Starting from delayed healthcare to LGBT personnel and sometimes denying the healthcare just because a person is gay, in many places gay men and others are compared to animals where you may come across the sign "gays and dogs not allowed". It took the world a very long time to get rid of discrimination on the major front (though it still prevails in regions) and this treatment does not help the situation. We all are mere people, so doing acts like denying public accommodation to members of LGBT just demarcates us into two separate species as if people are trying to call it as "people and non-people". This personal vendetta and dislike of some individuals just tends to become political hate making it difficult for gay GUYS, lesbian WOMEN, bisexual and trans people hard to survive.

What people really need to do is develop an incentive regarding all this stuff, understand what LGBT is REALLY about instead of running around here forming no way near to true concepts. Though we say, changes are being made and people are becoming more aware in the regard of LGBT community, the situation is better now but if we want to ensure equal treatment for gay people, there's a long road left to travel and we are just walking briskly, if we want to do this right: we need to get in on a ca

References

1. https://bestlifeonline.com/worst-lgbtq-stereotypes/

2. https://www.theatlantic.com/sexes/archive/2013/05/what-about-the-guys-who-do-fit-the-gay-stereotype/276407/

3. https://www.americanprogress.org/article/widespread-discrimination-continues-shape-lgbt-peoples-lives-subtle-significant-ways/

4. https://www.hrc.org/press-releases/new-fbi-hate-crimes-report-shows-increases-in-anti-lgbtq-attacks

5. https://en.m.wikipedia.org/wiki/LGBT_stereotypes

CHAPTER-5

LGBTQ+ Couples' Challenges

-Nidhi Jindal

nidhijindal956@gmail.com

The new era is marked by the news of gay weddings, with a flurry of same sex couples posting their happily ever after on the internet, they have started to take up the narrative of their lives with the portrayal of impeccable courage. Love is love and the same-sex community about the world is trying to prove the same by sticking to the people whom they love the most, defying gender, colour, and everything else. Same sex couples make up a great percentage of the society and despite of having quite a similar daily routine as most heterosexual couples, their social lives are marred with the influences of the dominant heterosexual culture and traditional expectations of gender roles within a relationship.

Most homosexual couples go through extreme rejection by their day-to-day support system and experience prejudice in different familial, legal, religious, economic, and social fields.

They're often discriminated against and are subjected to numerous types of mental and emotional torture by the society and its heterosexual members. As a minority, they undergo an immense amount of pressure which is forced onto them by the people around them.

From lack of parental recognition to reduced access to health care, these are some of the biggest issues facing LGBTQ families today:

1. Parental Recognition

Married heterosexual couples are recognized as the obvious legal guardians of their child, but homosexual couples are not given the same amount of legal respect when it comes to being recognized as parent of an individual. No matter what mode of pregnancy they approach, they are often not listed as parents on their child's birth certificate.

2. Access to Health Care

More sexual minorities are often found to be uninsured than straight people. This issue pans over access to all sorts of medical care, including gender-affirming medical care for transgender individuals.
And even when queer people are insured, they often do not get the same coverage of fertility options that heterosexual people do. Insurance policies are often framed in such ways that naturally make them applicable only to the heterosexual community.

3.Paid Parental Leave

While companies do have paid parental leave policies, those policies are often not inclusive of LGBTQ families. As stated earlier for health insurance policies, these too have been framed in ways that only make them applicable to heterosexual people.

4. Schools and Education

"While trying to deal with all the challenges of being a teenager, lesbian/gay/bisexual/transgender (LGBT) teens also have to deal with harassment, threats and violence directed at them on a daily basis.

LGBT youth are nearly twice as likely to be called names, verbally harassed or physically assaulted at school compared to their non-LGBT peers. Their mental health and education, not to mention their physical well-being, are at-risk."

6. Gender Roles

The already existing gender roles, when studied often portray women as the rational, emotional and healing body in a relationship while men are portrayed as instrumental, competitive, independent and emotionless. These gender roles then end up finding little application when it comes to same sex relationships.

Because, these gender roles don't really work in homosexual relationships, the similarity of biological sex and gender role conditioning allows couples to have a high level of friendly relationship in which they can understand each other deeply. They can understand that what features of their own sex make them happy. But due to being so different from the set societal norms, they're often forced to define their relationships the normal way, thus leaving them unanswerable to the question of "Who is THE MAN in the relationship?"

"Gender roles in non-heterosexual communities are a topic of much debate; some people believe traditional, heterosexual gender roles are often erroneously enforced on non-heterosexual relationships by means of heteronormative culture and attitudes towards these non-confirmative relationships."

7.   Stages Discrepancies

Generally, it takes so many years after the first awareness of the same sex infatuation for an individual to advance through a number of phases to fully reach a sexual minority identity. Stage discrepancies are very usual for so many same sex couples identified that many of these payers merge before partners have completed their own identity growth. Consequently, the members who undertake their individual sexual orientation development while simultaneously finding their way by accepting the challenges of an evolving relationship. Issues of betrayal and loyalty often occur, but rarely will couples see their hardships in terms of stage discrepancies. The result of these stage differences is conflict regarding the level of openness which is acceptable by family relationships for each and every partner for their employment community and friendship. Many relationships can overcome this conflict but some are unable to do so as far as heterosexual couples are concerned, the differences among the partners in their relationship stages are very common. For example, one wants more Liberty or separateness and the other is holding tightly or is fearful of differences or one begins to grow personally and the other perceives this as profligate or one wants more self-expression and the other wants to maintain harmony and avoid conflict. Conversely some lesbians and gay men are terrified if relationship becomes too close, since this reminds them of the suffocating closets of their earlier lives.

7. Violence

"Lesbian, gay, bisexual, and transgender (LGBT) people frequently experience violence directed toward their sexuality or gender identity.[1][2] This violence may be enacted by the state, as in laws prescribing punishment for homosexual acts, or by individuals. It may be psychological or physical and motivated by biphobia, gayphobia, homophobia, lesbophobia, and transphobia.

Influencing factors may be cultural, religious,[3][4][5] or political mores and biases.[6]"

Hate crimes against the queer community has always been a topic of debate and worry, different types of motivations lead several people to commit severe hate crimes against it. The past decade has seen a listless number of deaths and injuries that were caused by hate crimes against a simple community trying to exist.

It has been proved by various studies that the pride community is more likely to undergo violence than the heterosexuals.

"LGBT people are nearly four times more likely than non-LGBT people to experience violent victimization, including rape, sexual assault, and aggravated or simple assault, according to a new study by the Williams Institute at UCLA School of Law. In addition, LGBT people are more likely to experience violence both by someone well-known to the victim and at the hands of a stranger.

Researchers analysed data from the 2017 National Crime Victimization Survey, the first nationally representative and comprehensive criminal victimization data to include information on the sexual orientation and gender identity of respondents.

Results showed that, in 2017, LGBT people experienced 71.1 victimizations per 1,000 people, compared to 19.2 victimizations per 1,000 people for non-LGBT people. LGBT people had higher rates of serious violence victimization in almost every type of violent crime except robbery, which showed no significant difference between LGBT and non-LGBT people."

Conclusion

The challenges listed above mark a very small part of the torture that the members of the LGBTQ community undergo regularly. Thus, it's important to take a stand and to advocate better policies and improved laws.

The government needs to make sure that the laws made to support the LGBTQ community are followed perfectly across the country, leaving little chance of failure in execution. Folks also need to be made aware of these queer friendly laws once they are created.

Now that the pride movement has become more prominent across the world, it's time to stand for the movement and for all the LGBTQ+ individuals.

"Sociologist Mary Bernstein writes that -For the lesbian and gay movement, then, cultural goals include (but are not limited to) challenging dominant constructions

of masculinity and femininity, homophobia, and the primacy of the gendered heterosexual nuclear family (heteronormativity). Political goals include changing laws and policies to gain new rights, benefits, and protections from harm. Bernstein emphasizes that activists seek both types of goals in both the civil and political spheres."

And on the same hand, all the queer people also need to stand up and give their very best to this movement. It's important that as we try to fix the deep-rooted problems of the society, we also give rise to better generation who are well aware of how humans, no matter what sexual orientation they belong to, deserve an equal amount of respect.

References

- https://en.wikipedia.org/wiki/LGBT_movements#:~:text=Lesbian%2C%20gay%2C%20bisexual%2C%20and,of%20the%201960s%20and%201970s.
- https://www.mhanational.org/bullying-lgbt-youth
- https://williamsinstitute.law.ucla.edu/press/ncvs-lgbt-violence-press-release/

CHAPTER-6

Gender Assessment- "To Be or Not To Be"

-Srishti Upmanyu
archiesharma.sharma@gmail.com

It is common for people to think that the words 'sex' and 'Gender' are the same, but they mean different things. Human gender refers to their physical biology: being male or female. A person's gender identity, however, is a person's sense of identity - male, female, both or not. Gender identity is a profound concept of your gender. In some cases, a person's sexual identity may differ from his or her natural gender. Most children begin to express their sex when they are between 2 and 3 years old. They may do this by choosing toys, colors, and clothing that appeal to both boys and girls. By the time they are 3 years old, most children choose to play games that they think are appropriate for their gender, as well as other children of the same sex. For example, boys may play with trucks, and girls may play with dolls. Individual preferences may be similar to group preferences. However, changing a particular toy or clothing color can begin at an early age, which should be considered from the home itself. Demonstrating that color or a toy cannot make or break a particular sex can be a good way to start a healthy way to test Gender.

However, children do not begin to think of their sexuality as justified, or 'forever', until they are 6 or 7 years old. This happens when they are old enough to understand what sex means and are fully 'living' together. This means that they behave the way they think their environment expects them to behave. Gender roles are influenced by both our genes (part of our biology) and our environment. Children often copy the examples of adults like their parents or teachers. So, if a boy sees his father often doing chores such as car repairs, or a girl sees her mother doing most of the cooking, the child may think that these are 'men' and 'women' duties. A man can do whatever a woman can do no matter what the job. But segregation on the basis of Gender is what inequality arises. This chapter will look at the methods and challenges of Gender testing and how they should be fully accepted in society for society to be successful.

Although, it is important for children to know that girls can do well in sports, sports and school subjects such as maths, a community that often associates with boys. Likewise, it is important for boys to be free to pursue their own interests, regardless of what people think they should be.

Here are some things a person can do to help prevent your child from having sexual problems at an early age. (The stereotype is a common, but consistent, set of ideas and opinions about what it means to be a certain type of person. - Common roles, e.g., a female firefighter or a male nurse. Provide both girls and boys a variety of toys to play with, e.g., trucks, dolls, action figures and blocks. Let the kids choose their sports or hobbies. Let your child see you doing various activities that are not 'normal' in his or her sexuality. For example, my father could wash the clothes and my mother could cut the grass. Praise girls and boys in the same way. For example, if they are clean, courageous, kind, or physically active. Encourage children to make friends with both girls and boys. Try using gender-neutral terms such as 'firefighter' rather than 'firefighter'.

According to the World Health Organization (WHO), Gender refers to the social, emotional, and physical characteristics of women, men, girls, and boys. These include the habits, behaviors and roles associated with being a woman, a man, a girl or a boy, and the relationships between them. As with society, gender varies from person to person and can change over time. " Gender is intertwined but sexually different, referring to different biological and biological aspects of women, men and people of the opposite sex, such as chromosomes, hormones and reproductive organs. Gender and gender are related but different from gender identity. Sexual orientation refers to a person's deep, inner and individual feelings about sex, which may or may not be consistent with one's lifestyle or gender at birth. Understanding sex is not as easy as one might think. Gender is a spectrum. The ability to define who you are and to respect the community is one of the main reasons why sex is such a policy. A person should have the right to make his own decisions including the right to use any bathroom he feels comfortable using. However, we are not allowed to live in a world without sexist systems such as patriarchal and bisexualism. Has anyone ever wondered or asked who created the concept of blue for boys and pink for girls? Where do these ideas come from that boys do not cry or girls play with dolls? Such sexual relations are performed before the child is born. We have all played victims of this. Who hasn't bought a baby sex gift or attended a one-year-old pink princess party? Society distorts facts and wants people to express their masculinity or femininity. What is a feminist expression? What is the manifestation of manhood? Is it only physical? Do breasts prove to be a woman? Does being able to produce active sperm mean you are a real man? What about the mother of two children who had to have a double operation after being diagnosed with breast cancer? Is she no longer fit to be a woman because she has lost her breast? These and other questions are issues that are caused by false binary.

By using a public lens, we make the difference between sex and sex. Sex is the biological trait that societies use to classify people in the male or female class, whether by focusing on chromosomes, genitals or other physical records. When people talk about the differences between men and women, they tend to draw on sex - in the strong views of biology - rather than sex, which is an understanding of how society shapes our understanding of those stages of biology. Sex is very fluid - it can or does not depend on natural factors. Clearly, the concept that describes how societies determine and control sexual orientation; cultural definitions linked to the role of men and women; and how people understand their identity, which includes, but is not limited to, being male, female, transgender, heterosexual, heterosexual and other gender positions. Gender includes social norms, attitudes and activities that society considers more appropriate for one gender than another. Gender is also determined by what a person feels and does without regard to external stimuli or social obligations.

The sociology of gender examines how society influences our understanding and our perception of the distinction between "masculinity" (what society sees as "male" morality) and "femininity" (what society sees as "feminine" behavior). We examine how this, in turn, has impacted self-esteem and social behavior. We focus specifically on the power relations that follow the "gender system" established in a particular society, and how these changes over time can be important to us in terms of how we operate in a law-abiding society.

Gender and gender are not always compatible. "Cis-gender" refers to people whose natural physical makeup is similar to their own gender. This experience is different from being "transgender", in which the natural human sexuality is incompatible with their sexual identity. People who change genders will undergo a gender change that may involve changing the way they dress and present themselves (such as a change of name). Gender transplants may receive hormone therapy to facilitate the process, but not all transgender people will have surgery. Intersexuality refers to differences in sexual definitions associated with abnormal genitals, gonads, genitals, chromosomes or hormones. Transgender and intersexuality are categories of sex, not sex. Transgender people and lesbians have different sexual, attractive, and distinct traits as do the opposite sex. People can also be sex monitors, by drawing in a few sex positions or by not associating themselves with any particular (non-binary) sex; or they may be sexually transmitted (sexual fluids); or they may not accept sex (sex) categories. The third sex is often used by subject experts to describe cultures that is accepting of non-gender roles.

Gender is diverse too; is about sexual attraction towards someone, sexual habits and identity. Just as sex and sexuality are not always compatible, so is gender and sexuality. People can identify as a wide variety of genders from the opposite sex, to homosexuals or lesbians, to bisexuals, to professionalism, and so on. Asexuality is a term used when people do not feel sexually attracted. Some sexually active people can still form romantic relationships without sexual contact and be happy without any sexual experience.

Whatever we are and how we feel are two different things. And having a social responsibility for gender equality can be difficult for many. This is where social pressures can be a family or a workplace or an outreach. Social gender roles determine how a particular gender should behave, speak, act, speak, dress and behave in a way that is consistent with their gender. . For example, a woman should be caring, respectful and dignified and a man should be strong, aggressive and courageous. All communities, races, and cultures are expected to have a gender part, but they can vary greatly from one group to another group. For example, pink was considered a male color in the U.S. while blue is considered feminine. In India and many other countries in Southeast Asia, a boy is considered a man only when he begins to earn a good salary and a girl is considered a woman when she learns to care for her family. The stereotype can wreak havoc on the feelings of heterosexuals, resulting in heated debate over gender stereotypes. Gender stereotype as a general view or general opinion about the characteristics or features that they should or should have, or the roles that should be performed or should be performed by women and men. Sex stereotype is dangerous when it limits the ability of women and men to develop their skills, pursue their professional careers and make decisions about their health and their health plans. Different harmful ideas can be either hostile / evil (e.g., rational women) or appear positive (e.g. women exaggerate). For example, it has been based on the premise that women are more likely to be raised, that their responsibility to raise children is often up to them. " Sex stereotyping affects not only women and girls. Boys' exposure to sexual fantasies can be harmful in a number of ways, including emotional education, the pressure to appear masculine and powerful, and the choice of subjects and activities in which superstition is at their disposal. There is still a stigma attached to men taking on care roles, which could create additional barriers for boys in choosing 'non-traditional' subjects and compliance with public expectations informed by consistent views. Those who identify themselves as non-biased or transgender may have additional levels of social oppression, discrimination and harm as a result of non-compliance with perceived gender-based perceptions. In short, gender stereotypes negatively affect everyone by reducing their expression, development and progress based on strong social thinking and cultural norms.

Gender stereotyping refers to the practice of referring to a single woman or man for certain features, features or roles only for her own reason or her membership in a women's or men's social group. Sexual stereotyping is wrong if it leads to violations or violations of human rights and fundamental freedoms. An example of this, failure to make marital rape a crime based on the public perception that women are the property of men.

Sexual perceptions may be based on personality traits for example, women are often expected to be accepted and emotional, while men are generally expected to be confident and aggressive. Another common example of sexuality would be about domestic behaviour as some people expect women to take care of children, cook and clean the home, while men take care of finances, work in a car, and repair a home. Some stereotype brackets can be a job similar to Teachers and Nurses and are often associated with women and careers such as Pilot, Doctors and Engineers are often associated with men. A common myth about sex is physical appearance as women are expected to be thin and kind, while men are expected to be tall and muscular. Men and women are also expected to dress and groom themselves in an unusual way for their gender (men wearing trousers and short hair, women wearing dresses and cosmetics. Having a segregated class can lead to less communication between the sexes and can lead to greater discord among students. Also not only having an integrated education program can remove the concept of sexuality but also knowledge about human nature.

Human anatomy especially the reproductive system is the only system of human anatomy that is different for women and men. The reproductive organs are different from the male and the female but chromosomes and genes, which indicate that functional orange orangutans are very important. Chromosomes carry genes. Tiny pieces of DNA tell our cells what to do. Humans have 23 pairs of chromosomes. One pair contains sex chromosomes. They come in two forms: X and Y. Women have two Xs. Thus, when they share half of each chromosome pair with their offspring, the sex chromosome they provide will always be X. Men with X and Y. So, if a father shares the X chromosome with his child, he will make a girl (XX). If they share the Y chromosome, the baby will become a male (XY). Or at least, it usually is.

When it comes to sex, researchers have found that biology can be far more complex than just 'boy' or 'girl.' These people grow up to be what they look like in men. That is despite the fact that the presence of two X chromosomes means that they are female, at least biologically. It becomes even more difficult when gender identity comes into play. For more than 99 percent of the world's population, gender identity and natural gender will agree. Such a person is called a cisgender. (The Latin prefix means "on the same side.") But a small percentage of people have differences in gender. Some of these people grow up feeling that they do not have sex all over the world - including their parents and doctors - who see them as their own. This experience is called transgender. The word transgender is different from transgender, which means that a person is attracted to both men and women. People who change genders may appear to be male or female. But for some unexplained reason, they feel as if - and, finally, they say they know - they are of the opposite sex. Some may even identify with both sexes.

Hyper femininity is a trait in which a woman expresses herself through an exaggerated version of the stereotype such as inaction, ignorance, softness, sexual ignorance, kindness and acceptance. These symptoms make a woman less independent and more submissive to the opposite sex. Since the roles have been placed on him in an orderly manner without going out of it, he is familiar with the methods of the role and does not readily accept the change so easily. When women stick to traditional gender norms usually when they get something by doing so, such as in cultural backgrounds with financial benefits. The girl poker players of "Texas Hold Em" use this strategy for winning by distracting in a certain "female" way- they try to be sensually sexual, the dumb damsel in distress to get things done. They feel that if they try to flirt, they will be allowed to marry and be considered "prostitutes." Poker, if we view in terms of skill-set, appears to be not favourable for either of the genders but in reality, somehow it has become associated with masculinity. If someone says a casino, you'll imagine men playing poker with women sticking by the sides of the winning man. The plays that male-players use in the game represent sexual nature of abuse directed to women so the female-players think that they must adhere to those to get the job done. This response of women "reproduces their racist ideas" even though they think it will help them to win. But while playing as men, women lose credibility as opponents as they prove the whole point of gender-biases in the game by being aggressive. When we look at the crack coca dealers who are women, they represent the same category where they cling to 'women traits' for finance. A study found that it was rather convenient for women to take up this job while their kids stay at the home. The very fact that keeps women from being aggressive and using threats (being men) is that they realise their way of doing this must be more professional to keep up with the society. So, to uplift the status of woman, traditional, and mother- they have to demarcate their work from the supposed work life. This separation is considered a benefit to their working life, not to mention the obvious beneficiary in the home. These two scenarios are opted by women because they are financially sound. On the other hand, you have to be acting in 'masculine' or 'feminine' ways in order to get accepted by some cultural groups. A prime example to this is seen clearly when we look at women in gangs involved in criminal activity and also how they start in them in the first place. A study was conducted by Miller about the girls who are part of these gangs alongside the roles they are given. Her discussions with 20 girls in heterosexual gangs and 26 in no gang at all were in depth studies. The main reason of joining for them is that by joining one they are offered protection from the others. One way to deal with the men who aren't part of the group is to be in a gang with majority of male members. Though to point out the irony of the situation, it was abusive and even in some cases lead to sexual harassment. If that is not enough, there is a male initiated process for getting accepted in a gang - "beat in" where who have to prove your toughness and reliability of even being a part of the group. If one is looking for another way in, you have to "connect" with the group's best man, the leader or anyone he selects. This route is only available to female sisters or members of a gang. This method offers even higher protection from the members withing the group as if you do harass or abuse the woman, you'd be crossing the line with that man in the higher-ranking. For a woman, there's always the way where you can have sex with the several of the gang members indicating availability at all times for sex. Women are considered weakest and lowest in a gang by males and females alike. Miller's research has found that the type of circumcision chosen is the basis for decision about their role as a member in the gang and what all things they have the liberty to do. You are prohibited from any participation in acts of high violence if you are a woman. When it comes to sexes, the boundaries are clear in the groups. To top it all off, the punishments if you are 'women' are prevailing. For example, one girl told a story about a violent gang that abused her rival wife. Sexual abuse of women as a form of punishment or violence is only found in female members because of their natural gender. The risk of abuse is higher for women in mixed sex groups. The difference in such groups is that they are established in a comparatively more formal manner. The leadership works in yet more different manner, between sexes in the gang moreover, between men and between women. Women also use self-defence strategies in those cultural groups. The masculinity in some women is a trait which allows themselves to be perceived differently than "women" women. This distinction creates a platform where men always top the women, and are treated in obvious better ways. This makes some things abundantly clear, that women if present in hypermasculine cultures as such need to be more mas6culine- if they fail to practice this masculinity, they aren't accepted nor respected, even if they lose any femininity due to explicit dichotomy. However, just as in every other case in the world the exceptions are present for sure, such as those for women in the Texas Hold Em poker team who found that playing the ''not so sharp girl' theory benefited them. Majority of these females are not trying to get accepted as a part of the society but are there only because of their 'interactions' with the male gender. Because of these clear differences between men and women, more self-defence occurs so that men can show that they are part of the group they are trying to belong to. The gender-based categorisation, as indicated in studies, is not present in all subcultures as some are free of it. For example, a study that examined female methamphetamine users, retailers, and manufacturers found that the system in these societal aspects have got nothing to do with sex. In these situations, the roles are assigned on abilities and talent on an individual level, where women users were low and the produces were high. The male domination is prevalent in power-positions as shown in polls, such as political positions or corporate leadership positions. The workplace, if we look at the numbers, has a women majority but these studies help understand the authority and power play situations. The study shows the jobs such as firefighting and police officers and also military which require necessary physical and mental masculinity. For obvious reasons, gender inequality is seen as a problem in jobs that are demanding physical strength and have a violence-based core.

Females who work in male roles can often cause feelings of doubt about their co-workers. For example, female police officers are subject to scrutiny because of the belief that women are softer than men, which affects a female police officer and the community at large. There is concern that women cannot use guns like men. The male police officers reported that they thought it was unlikely that the female police officers would be equal to them in terms of job-concerning skills and that their skills were poor which could lead to more male police officers. Overall, the issue being raised about is that women are unable to handle dangerous situations. Similar data was presented about women firefighters, whose study found that they could not carry their weight and slow down male firefighters. However, after working with female firefighters and realizing their potential, these perceptions have been found to diminish. Women gave themselves higher scores of competence than their male counterparts. Men were concerned that women would receive special treatment at work, while women thought they did not and should not receive special treatment. These findings indicate that there is a clear difference between the way women perceive themselves and the way men view themselves.

Like Hyper femininity there is the term Hyper masculinity for men. A man who portrays a view of violence as masculinity, a view of danger as pleasurable and arousing, and the indifference of women and the perception of emotional expression as feminine traits that reflect the height of masculine sexuality. These types of sex are dangerous as the older woman will face violence and apart from independence on the other hand the Hyper Masculine man is the one who incites violence against the woman. To conclude, on researching about the gender equality in the workplace indicates clearly how women in male-dominated work-spaces are often looked down upon, should be more discriminating, and should not always be held in high esteem by their male counterparts. This takes up to something else because women have these conditions that are connected together according to their gender. These findings also indicate that gender is a part of almost every communication people engage in on a daily basis, even in their work. When women are employed in full-time or male-dominated jobs, they have a much higher level of sexuality because they are informed about their sexuality through sexual orientation. This situation can have real consequences for sexual harassment in the workplace. It is possible that women in these jobs are less likely to report abuse because they feel it can make a person feel unfamiliar with them, and face the worst. Another way to combat this experience is to have more women in jobs that are often filled by men for example, Law, Engineering, pilots, Defense etc.

"Cultural attitudes and gender stereotypes often regard women as inferior to men, or they say men should dominate women," said Navi Pillay, the UN High Commissioner for Human Rights. "These attitudes can be so entrenched and deeply ingrained in society that they are almost invisible - without their consequences. Because they continue to be racist, violent and humiliating." According to the World Health Organization, gender inequality begins at birth. Provides a report published by WHO in 2020 in India, too many young girls, especially those from economically backward families, face a lot of sexual discrimination in education and workplace, child marriage and pregnancy, sexual violence and neglected domestic help as a result of the ongoing epidemic. Even before the epidemic, girls were more likely than boys to never set foot in class. Conflict, poverty and other forms of social inequality also exacerbate gender inequality in education. Girls living in conflict-affected countries, for example, are 2.5 times more likely to drop out of school than boys. An estimated 9.7 million children were at risk of being expelled from school by the end of 2020, with girls facing increased risk. Child marriage is a form of gender-based violence that results in and promotes gender inequality and gender discrimination. Experts predict that the COVID-19 epidemic will be postponed to delay 25 years of progress, leading to a decline in child marriage. In fact, a study by Save the Children revealed that some 2.5 million girls are at risk of getting married by 2025 because of the epidemic — a dramatic increase in child marriage rates for nearly three decades. Gender-based violence is a global phenomenon in all economic and social groups. Although boys and girls are badly affected, girls are at greater risk. It is estimated that 1 in 3 women worldwide has experienced physical or sexual abuse in their lifetime, especially at the hands of their partners. Types of violence may include: preterm sex, genital mutilation, neglect, female genital mutilation, rape, child marriage, forced prostitution, honourable murder and stabbing. Many of these gross violations of human rights have been used as weapons of war worldwide. Refugee children are at high risk. There are currently 152 million child exploits worldwide. Employment of children makes it difficult for children to go to school or reduce their attendance, which puts them at risk of falling behind by their peers. Boys and girls are affected differently by child abuse and parental decisions are often influenced by broader social norms regarding the different roles they should play at home and in the community. Girls are more likely to be responsible for household chores while boys are more likely to be involved in hazardous activities such as construction. Girls are usually excluded from school before boys and are more likely to experience sexual exploitation and slavery. Therefore, to say that gender inequality occurs only after a certain age may be an understatement as many studies and reports have shown that gender inequality occurs from an early age.

Emerging constructions based on gender role expectations also emerge as inequalities. While speculative gender perceptions incline to be more precise in predicting the differences between women and men at the social level at the individual level, theories based on the common view are the best and most likely and most inaccurate sexism. For example, although men are generally more powerful than women, one cannot assume that all male members of the opposite sex are more independent than all other members of the female group. In addition to these potential costs, observers often rely on gender roles for the emerging role of individual women and men because gender roles require less cognitive resources, and because divisive information is not always available. Understanding how gender roles influence group behavior and adaptability is important in order to understand how gender diversity affects group performance. Each team and each organization usually aims to hire the best (i.e., the most knowledgeable, competent, competent) person in the job or profession, with the same responsibilities assigned based on the person's ability and ability. However, in the focus on finding the best person, there is a caveat, because the viewer's point of view and personal evaluation are largely based on the thinking and beliefs of the industry "Scullen et al., 2000". The expectations of gender roles are a major source of such bias and beliefs. For example, meta-analytical evidence suggests that men are preferred over women with equal skills in male-dominated careers (but not women who are typed or integrated) "Koch et al., 2015". These findings are consistent with the scarcity model and the role of co-operative roles that show that men are more likely to be hired and elected, or promoted to leadership positions because men's roles are better or more equal. it goes hand in hand with a leadership role in the eyes of the audience.

Ironically, it is the misrepresentation of women in leadership positions that ultimately reinforces the role of gender in men being better qualified for leadership positions, as long as women are not given the opportunity to show their worth. Indeed, social role theory and state-building theory suggest that the mere ideas of men holding positions of leadership and women are overly represented in supporting (e.g., managing) or developing (e.g., caregiver) roles created, strengthened, and continue to support the belief. . or to expect that men are better suited to agency and leadership roles and that women are more qualified to support and develop roles. Such an impact on the expected gender role not only applies to the allocation of positions but also to many other allocation and decision-making processes in organizations. Consider, for example, performance ratings, award prizes, and promotional decisions. It is no coincidence that such analysis and decisions are also influenced by expectations about the role of gender, given that high performance testing may result in higher wages, additional promotions, and more opportunities for prominence, employment, or debt. Gender expectations can therefore shape the allocation of responsibilities, duties, and responsibilities by affecting early performance appraisal, which is also important in determining who gets the job.

If you look at the effects of the expected gender role in the consistent distribution of tasks, activities, and responsibilities (i.e., over time), those effects may seem small or non-existent. However, because of the harmonious nature of distribution and decision-making processes, the result of the accumulation over time may well explain why the female half is often lower when a person rises a hierarchical ladder in organizations "Martell et al., 1996; Agars, 2004; Ridgeway , 2011 ".

In short, we suggest that gender roles shape decisions about role roles, responsibilities, and responsibilities, such as gender roles that are expected to generally support and strengthen. Men are more likely to be selected for jobs, occupations, and responsibilities that are relevant to men's roles, and women are more likely to be selected for jobs, occupations, and responsibilities that are relevant to women's roles. After gender reassignment, gender roles and expectations can be strengthened and strengthened.

All humanity is made up of many different people, they come up with many different ways of life and they have a very different way of looking at the world as it comes. Therefore, it is important to consider this unique difference because it may cause some security risks, and also because they can often be used to improve the condition of those affected. By systematically implementing the Age, Gender and Diversity (AGD) approach, aid stakeholders want to ensure that all people in the affected communities have access to their rights equally. Applying the AGD method is not an addition: it is a key element of fair and equitable protection. By analyzing the magnitude of AGD as integrated personal factors, we are better able to better understand the security risks associated with the capabilities of individuals and communities, and to address and support them more effectively. By promoting respect for diversity as an enrichment for any society, we are advancing progress towards a state of absolute equality. Equality means respecting everyone. It includes the promotion of equal opportunities for people with different needs and skills as well as direct, measurable actions against inequality and discrimination. The AGD approach can also be defined as: Age refers to the different stages of a person's life cycle. It is important for protection systems to be aware of where people are in their life cycle as their skills and needs change over time. Age affects, and can enhance, or diminish, a person's ability to exercise his or her rights. Prevention risks affect a person differently depending on age.

Gender refers to the socially constructed roles of women, girls, men and boys. Gender roles are studied, evolved over time, and vary within and between cultures. Gender often defines the roles, responsibilities, barriers, opportunities and rights of women, girls, men and boys in any situation. Gender equality refers to the equal enjoyment of their rights, responsibilities and opportunities and means that the interests, needs and priorities of each gender are respected.

Diversity means different values, attitudes, cultural views, beliefs, ethnic background, nationality, sexual orientation, gender identity, ability, health, social status, ability and other personal characteristics. Although age and gender are common to all individuals, some factors vary from person to person. This difference should be noted, understood and important by the emergency services players in each emergency situation to ensure the safety of all affected people.

The UNHCR Age, Gender and Diversity Policies have been developed by the UNHCR- United High Commission for Refugees which highlights the fact that people have equal rights and enjoy equality and participation in the different countries to which they have migrated. There are also other ways to have a socially friendly environment. Gender neutrality is one way to overcome gender inequality. Also, having gender-neutral games for both women and men can reduce the challenge of gender bias testing.

Apart from the above-mentioned reason, there is a very important reason for the misunderstanding of the word Gender and Sex. The word Sex means the male and female parts of a person's genitalia. But the definition of Gender is different than the social issues that made a person feel it. Gender may differ from one person to another. Rather it will be what one feels mentally and naturally. Gender has a very different perspective than sex. Gender cannot be boxed for others like Men or Women. Having a two-dimensional perspective on sex has made some people feel isolated and uncomfortable in expressing their views in public. Some men who do not see themselves as men as they should be, like to dress feminine in public and are called names such as cross-dresser and she-male (especially in Southeast Asian countries). On the other hand, Women who do not consider themselves women as women should be socially commonly referred to as Tomboy (in many Western countries and cultures) and known as spinster without research or discovery. Such pronouns make it easier for people who have not been sexually tested to get into trouble and create a stigma attached to it.

Sex is NOT sex, but we still exchange it. Applying these to formulating health policies and Health programs can have serious consequences. Having an open mind about the differences between the two can help the government make better health policies and programs. In conclusion, feeling like you're crawling on one's skin to feel real is something no one should ever feel like getting through. Being able to relax physically or mentally in your own skin should be the most important human right. or for those who don't fit well into the boy-girl divisions , these ongoing references to the two groups of men and women can be reserved. And if we talk about the ones who do identify as male and female, these persistent reminders about sexuality can have a profound effect. Constantly separating people from men and women can make us feel that men and women are very different from who we really are. True and true reversal and rearrangement are necessary to have a clear idea of what the true meaning of sexuality is and how it affects the human race.

"Even what might be considered nonsense language can have far-reaching negative effects on the way we see the world," writes Lera Boroditsky, professor of Cognitive Sciences at UCSD. In a few of the languages out there, even the objects are categorized as male or female, you find that this distinction affecting people's perception of something. For example, when German and Spanish-speaking people were asked to identify a key, their responses differed, with the man in German and the woman in Spanish. Germans used masculine nouns such as "rough", "sorrated", "hard" and "iron" to describe the key, and Spanish speakers used feminine nouns such as "small", "shiny", "gold". and "complex. Responses were delayed for the word "bridge", feminine in German and masculine in Spanish. Clearly it was found that sexualizing and assigning gender to object leads to less gender equality.

Although English contains less sex than other languages, there are still many gender references. For those trying to be more sensitive to sex in their everyday language, there are a few good places to start. According to Vitor Shereiber, Project Manager for Babbel language learning app, "Most languages don't have gender pronouns." For example, it does not have gender as a category of Turkish and Indonesian pronouns. The use of the words "he" and "she" in English requires each person to be assigned a gender.

You cannot always make out the other person's pronouns just by the their appearance as a whole. Asking and using someone else's pronouns is a way to show respect for our sexual orientation. Shereiber says that for those who do not define themselves as men or women, the unity of "they" still continues. The American Dialect Association used the term "they" for the decade 2010-2019, and in 2019 the Merriam-Webster dictionary changed their definition so that "they" can be used for "a person with non-binary ownership". "

So, when it comes to one person, is it correct to say "you" or "you"? Merriam-Webster recommends "they" as they are probably the way we feel most comfortable speaking and hearing.

While the word "they" can easily be incorporated into your everyday speech, there are a number of other gender-neutral pronouns like "zie" and "sie" that people may choose to use. Be sure to ask others about their pronoun preference before making any assessments. Swedes have adopted the nickname "chicken" for sexual neutrality, and kindergartens and kindergartens are reportedly using the term to help children "grow up without feeling the effects of sexism."

In conclusion, making a person of any gender, feeling inferior or being exploited is not something that humanity should go down. And being born of a certain sex will never make a person superior or inferior as a person who is not bound to a particular gender. Perhaps a person can gain a lot as an individual or as a society, if he has the right to choose which sex, he wants more than what he deserves in the society in which he lives. Social norms can never make a person grow to full potential if he or she has not been raised in a safe and secure society without fear of exploitation.

Works Cited:

- [1] Stoet, G., & Geary, D. C. (2018). The paradox of gender equality in science, technology, engineering, and mathematics education. Psychology, 29, 581-593.
- [2] Charles, M., Harr, B., Cech, E., & Hendley, A. (2014). Who likes math where? Gender differences in the attitudes of eighth graders around the world. International Studies in Sociology of Education, 24, 85-112. ; Hendley, A., & Charles, M. (2015). Gender segregation in higher education. Emerging Trends in Social and Behavioural Sciences, 1-11.
- [3] Corrigendum: The Gender-Equality Paradox in Science, Technology, Engineering, and Mathematical Education. (2020). Psychology, 31, 110-111.
- [4] Richardson, S. S., & Bruch, J. (2020, February 12). Bizarre monkey business with gender equality: Or, a way to tell false stories about the achievement of women at the national level in STEM. GenderSci Blog.
- [5] Richardson, S. S., Reiches, M. W., Bruch, J., Boulicault, M., Noll, N. E., & Shattuck-Heidorn, H. (published). Is there a paradox of gender equality in science, technology, engineering, and mathematics (STEM)? Comments in the study of Stoet and Geary (2018). Psychological Science.
- [6] Ellemers, N. (2018). Sexual orientation. Annual Psychology Review, 69, 275-298.

CHAPTER-7

Freedom for Nature-bound Roles in Shobha De's Selected Novels

-Dr. Rashmi Gupta[1]

& Dr. Renu Rani[2]
(rashmigupta77@gmail.com)

This chapter analyses how Shobha De's women characters do not have a strong need to acknowledge the ideological images imposed by patriarchal structure; rather, they want equal treatment in all spheres of life. Generally, in coital relationship, due to an innate feeling of superiority and arrogance, men do not care to know the feelings of women. That is why, De's women lack interest in having sexual relationships with inconsiderate men. The present paper analyses the lesbian relationship predominant in the cosmopolitan way of life.

Lesbian feminism is a cultural movement and critical stance that encourages women to direct their energy, attention, relationships, and activities toward other women rather than males, and frequently promotes lesbianism as a natural extension of feminism. Lesbian feminism is a subgroup of feminism that evolved at the intersection of the women's movement, homosexual rights activism, and the sexual revolution in the mid-to-late twentieth century. Lesbian feminists believe that same-sex relationships are valid and that their lesbian identity may be used to establish community and take collective action. Lesbian feminism criticizes heterosexuality and male supremacy as "normal" and offers a counter-narrative.

Karuna and Anjali of Socialite Evenings, and Malini of Starry Nights, do not have desire for sex with their husbands who are so unresponsive and insensitive towards their feelings. Anjali narrates to Karuna about her disinterest in sexual encounters with her husband Abe: "I just switch off and think of other things. Sometimes I pick the black heads on his back or concentrate on my schedule for the next day" (SE, 44). In Malini's intercourse with Akshay, "She hated his breath, his favourite cologne, the curly hair in his armpits . . ." (SN, 47). For satisfying his hunger, "She'd 'allow' him to make love, as she lay there impassively, with a martyred expression on her face, . . . While he was doing his 'business' she would go over the words of a favourite ghazal in her mind and plan her next day's schedule. It was amazing, the number of mental chores she accomplished while Akshay was grunting away . . ." (SN, 46). Thus, these women show their hatred in having sex with their insensitive husbands by being frigid and indifferent. Beauvoir observes: ". . . in bed the woman punishes the male for all the wrongs she feels she has endured, by offering him an insulting coldness" (1983, 413).

Sometimes, when a woman wishes to escape from male domination in sexual relationships, she tries to get sexual-fulfilment by other means against the traditional norms and moral codes of conduct. In this way, the women characters of Shobha De, against their nature-bound roles, seek alternatives for their sexual gratification. In Starry Nights, though Aasha has several sexual relations with men for the sake of 'the greatest orgasm,' she feels great joy only in lesbian experience with the Thai girls. Similarly, in her lesbian relationship with her journalist friend Linda, too, she gets a pleasant feeling. In this context, Linda's words show how much woman has resentment for man's violent act in physical relationship. While having lesbian relationship, Linda remarks: "'THIS is love, understand? This is love-making, not what those bastards do to our bodies.' Aasha Rani was lulled to sleep by Linda's fingers stroking her. Yes, she thought, this is what it should be tender, beautiful and erotic. In a way it could never be with a man" (SN, 80). Thus Aasha, for the first time, enjoys sexual encounter with Linda as an equal partner. In this relationship, she does not feel a sense of humiliation or guilt. Likewise, Surekha, in Snapshots, is happier to spend her life with her lesbian friend, Dolly, than with her husband with whom she feels "dissatisfaction with her sex-life" (SS, 158). The major cause behind this type of relationship is woman's reaction against man's insensitivity and arrogance. Therefore, these women declare, "that they have no more need of men socially than sexually" (Beauvoir 1983, 443).

In the same vein, two major women characters of Strange Obsession, Minx and Amrita, involve themselves in lesbian relationships. Amrita, "an attractive, ambitious, glamorous model" (SO, 2), comes to Bombay to put her foot in the modelling world where she attracts a bold but mysterious lady, Minx. Minx candidly reveals her expectation: "I'm your friend. And I want you to be mine. That's all'" (SO, 28). Initially, Amrita shows no interest in maintaining relationship with Minx. She even rejects Minx's proposal of staying together: "'Forget it! We can never be friends or lovers or anything. I don't know what it is that you want out of me. But whatever you're after, you won't get it'" (SO, 22-23). Despite the friction in her relationship with Minx, as purposeful young woman, she does not want a break off in her career; hence, she hides it from others. Because if she lets her family know this ugly truth, then she would not be allowed to stay for her career in Bombay and, thus, her decision to find out her true self and vocation will not materialize. Further, she thinks that it is her personal problem and she should solve it on her own. Moreover, there are occasions when Minx's outbursts are too convincing for Amrita, for instance:

'Why? Why does it make sick? Why should it? Because I belong to the same sex? Is that my only sin? You find it sickening to accept my love. . . . But what about that animal Rover's love? That's OK. You enjoy that. How come? And don't tell me 'because they are men. And it's normal.' Bullshit! There is nothing abnormal about my feelings for you. It is your problem that you have hang-ups" (SO, 44).

In a sense, Minx's words represent the feminist outcry and reveal the resentment against this social foundation in which sexual relationship between man and woman has social and legal validity, whereas love between two females is considered strange and mean. Minx proclaims to Karan, a photographer and a lover of Amrita: "And what's abnormal about mine? Just because I am a woman does it mean my love is inferior to yours? Or to any man's?" (SO, 163). These words reflect that Minx does not consider a woman's love for a woman in any way inferior to a man's love for a woman.

Minx even acts like a man and shows how without masculine help, she is self-sufficient and capable of taking care of herself and her friends. Amrita's first meeting with Minx happens when Minx offers Amrita timely help. Then, Minx introduces her friends to Amrita in a manly way: "'This is Kallu. That's Kaniya. He's Albert and this is his friend, Pagla.' After a pause, she added, 'Don't worry . . . they're my boys. Safe. . . . Local dadas,' she said by way of an explanation, 'but loyal to me'" (SO, 6). Minx wants to save Amrita under her protection and, like a man, she tries to prove her power to Amrita by performing some dangerous acts. In the novel, both Minx and Amrita are eager to create strong positions for them in a highly male-dominated society. De suggests that since Minx's idea to seek her 'self' by behaving like a man cannot be approved by Indian society, that is why her character meets with death at the end of the novel. It also indicates that a woman cannot get self-importance merely by blindly imitating man but only by gaining the true knowledge of self-value. In this novel, as it has been pointed out already, initially Amrita was not interested in lesbian relationship, but when Minx concocts a story of rape by her father, she begins to sympathize with her and develops genuine interest in her.

In the novel, Sisters, the major women characters, Mikki and Alisha, are shown as highly ambitious, confident and career conscious women who reject the passive image of traditional woman. The novel also projects the repulsion of women against any social injustice and indiscrimination. After the sudden death of her parents, Mikki, who is just about twenty years old, finds herself with the responsibility of running her father's industries, which are already in the red. She "a rich, little, orphan" (S, 13) is left alone and vulnerable "like a small mouse with vultures all around just waiting to pounce on her" (S, 27). However, she has enough courage to accept all those responsibilities. About dealing with all the matters of Hiralal Industries, Ramankaka advises her: "leave these serious matters to me. I am there to handle them . . . you will make things difficult for yourself if you do things without consulting me" (S, 30). However, asserting her own self, she emphatically declares: "Thank you for your advice, Ramankaka. . . . I can't change my sex, unfortunately. That is the one thing all of you will have to accept. . . . My genes are the same as my father's even if my gender isn't. I am determined not to let the companies go by default. I will learn whatever I have to and I will hire whoever I think fit" (S, 30-31).

In this way, Mikki challenges the orthodox notions of Indian society, which considers woman a weakling and unfit for creativity. Although after her parents' death, she is burdened with heavy responsibilities, she does not lose her moral courage. Boldly, she prevents her maidservant from weeping: "Gangubai, please stop that . . . what has happened has happened" (S, 2). Being a woman, she is not afraid of facing the difficulties of life, but she has a high spirit to win against all odds. In this regard, De's women subscribe to Germaine Greer's view that

"The female body is not our enemy but our strength: it is not our sex that confines us but the hatred and disgust of others for our sex. . . .. That future may be almost upon us, but it will not bring liberation unless it has been desired and designed by women themselves. Refusing to be defined, discriminated against and disadvantaged because of our female biology should not be confused with a demand to be deprived of it." (1999, 325).

In her determination to save her father's companies at any rate, Mikki accepts the suggestion of her cousin, Shanay, and requests for finance from her fiancé, Navin. Yet Navin, as a 'Mamma's boy', cannot take decision on his own. He organizes a meeting where his "presence was merely decorative" (S, 81) and the decision is to be taken by his mother. Further, Mikki feels humiliated when she is treated inferior by Navin's mother, who tells other members: "Bachchi hai. She is young and new to all this. We must encourage her, now that she has joined the business community" (S, 81). True, as an executive, Mikki needs help from others to save her father's companies, but for that, she is not going to let herself dominated or underrated as lower being by others.

Hence, Mikki shows her assertive and strong character and finally declares to call off her engagement with Navin: "She leaned towards Shanay and said, 'Cheer up. It is not the end of the world, you know, we will find someone else to help us out. . . . The engagement was off, she stated simply, without going into elaborate explanation. . . . Surprisingly, Mikki did not feel bitter at all. . . . She raised her glass and clinked it with Shanay's 'To life', she said" (S, 82).

Ultimately, the new woman's essential urge is to be treated as an equal partner to man. Mikki, as a new woman, feels a strong need to be understood as a person of her own values, that is why, even in an atmosphere of deep distrust and mutual hostility, she is not ready "to take orders from anyone" (S, 71). When Navin lets her down, she begins to search other ways to win in her fight. Moreover, in her attempt, she decides to marry Binny Malhotra, a businessman of middle age. Again, she has to struggle against the constraints of this patriarchal society of being a woman. In her life, she wants someone to stand by her so that she can emerge as a winner from all the struggles in her life. However, Binny's idea is only to have a wife who merely functions as a decorative piece for his house. He makes his views brutally clear to Mikki: "Your life is perfect. Your job is to look beautiful. I told you that when I married you. Buy clothes. Buy jewellery. Go to the beauty parlor. Play bridge. Learn golf. Attend cooking classes. That's all. But no questions you don't have the right and none of this cheeky business. I will not tolerate it" (S, 116).

Mikki, who intends to stick to her ideological role of a wife, is ready to "give him every bit of herself, her body, her mind, her soul"(S, 109). But not at that level where she has to obliterate her own self, and mutely accept all the decisions imposed on her by her husband. However, because of the incompatible relationship with her self-absorbed husband, she, finally, decides to break the shackles of marriage and tries to seek her life's mission in taking up the responsibility of her father's industry and of her sister Alisha.

In this same novel, Mikki's counterpart, Alisha, is born of Seth Hiralal's illegal relationship with his mistress, Anjanaben. Having known the death of her father from newspaper and seeing the reference of Mikki as his only child, Alisha mocks: "and what about me? What am I? A puppy? A kitten? A pet?" (S, 3). Her awakened spirit is not ready to admit the defeat. She dares to attend her father's funeral in spite of her mother's objection. De describes: "But she was not going to hide any longer. She would go and face them all . . . she was going to Shanty Kutir as Seth Hiralal's other daughter, the one he had fathered but never acknowledged" (S, 5). She does not like to belittle her identity of being an illegal daughter. However, Mikki, who is happy to have someone reliable like Alisha, is determined to "win her over" (S, 16). Although Mikki meets her and requests her to accept her friendship, Alisha, who does not have any remorse for being an illegitimate daughter, retorts: "We may not be rich like you, but we have our self-respect. We value our independence" (S, 16). Actually, Alisha thinks that Mikki is trying to buy her and her mother. Hence, she rejects any sympathy, but demands a rightful place for her in the society. So, she rebuffs Mikki's help when she declares: "I don't need your fucking charity. Get it? And hung up"(S, 16). Not accepting an anomalous identity, Alisha is confident and firm to establish herself as a recognized person. In this way, in a party when someone tries to make a comparison between her and Mikki, Alisha screams: "Don't ever say that to me again. Get it? I am me. Alisha Mehta. I have nothing to do with that other female" (S, 25). The novel thus reveals Alisha's passion to find her identity by protesting against any inferior position given to her due to her illegal birth. When Ramankaka, who handles all the money affairs in Hiralal industries, discloses her father's will in a vague way, Alisha curtly remarks to Ramanbhai: "'Whatever it is that you've come here for, get on with it fast. We don't need your charity. We aren't beggars. However, my father owed us some responsibility and I hope you have come here to discharge it on his behalf" (S, 47).

By and large, Alisha does not want to be taken for granted for anything in her life. She is resentful of the senseless rules, which allows a man to enjoy illicit relationships but looks down upon his illegitimate children. She hates Mikki because both are daughters of same father, but Mikki has respect in society owing to her socially approved birth. Despite her hard-earned success, she could not come out of Mikki's shadow. In the words of De:

"With each encounter, Alisha's rage against the injustice of her situation only grew. She promised herself that one day the balance would alter in her favour. One day, people would feel sorry for Mikki. One day, she, Alisha, would be on top of the situation, looking down on all those people who didn't give her the time of the day. They would, she swore, oh yes, they would. They owed her that much. But first, she'd finish Mikki." (S, 100).

Alisha wants to avenge her father's injustice to her by taking revenge on Mikki. Thus in order to belittle her at any cost, she buys a bungalow near to Mikki's, and in order to show herself superior to her, she wants a marble plaque which says Alisha's Hideaway in gold letters. Alisha's sexual encounters are also a result of her abhorrence for the hypocritical society that gives importance only to Mikki. Hence, she has physical relationship with Navin, a former lover of Mikki, for the only reason that "Mikki had him" (S, 20). Even in her sexual intercourse with him, "She was visualizing Mikki doing the same thing to Navin. . . . She wanted to obliterate any memory Navin might have retained of his love-making with the woman she hated" (S, 123).

Nevertheless, Alisha considers her mother's life so important, because if she loses her mother, she will be also 'parentless' like Mikki; but having her mother "she wanted to be one up on Mikki, on that score at least" (S, 126). All these examples related to Alisha illustrate her earnest desire to be identified with a valuable and respectable self. Whatever she does, whether right and wrong, she passionately aspires to find her own self as precious as Mikki's. So rejecting the passive traditional image, she, with confidence, reliability, unshakable strength and toughness, tries to establish a firm sense of identity in this patriarchal society.

Bursting with self-confidence, De's women often adopt challenging, dangerous, and unethical acts only to show men that women also have courage and power to do so, which are socially understood to be the prerogative of men alone. In this way, Nisha boldly allows Iqbal, a painter, to paint her naked body for the cover page of 'Plume', a magazine. He starts taunting her: "Body Acchi hai, yaar pretty good. Kapde utaar do . . . go on, take your clothes off" (SD, 61). Without feeling any sense of shame or humiliation, Nisha, accepts his provocation by responding affirmatively: "Sure, why not?" (SD, 61).

In Snapshots, Reema remembers her school day sexual experience with Raju, her boy friend. She could never forget it; not because she enjoyed it too much "but the expression in Raju's eyes as he raised himself over her body like a conqueror" (SS, 93). At that time, she felt like a loser as he crushed her 'self'. She also concludes that it is not only Raju, but also every man with superior outlook, considering himself the master of female sexuality. After so many years of her physical relationship with him, she finds no point in living a very restricted life of social and moral conduct. Now, "She'd turned into an unfeeling, mechanical woman" (SS, 93). If promiscuous life can sooth the suppressed self, then De's women do not hesitate to come out of conventional codes of morality.

References

➢ Beauvoir, Simone De. (1983). The Second Sex. Trans. H. M. Parshley. Harmondsworth: Penguin Books.
➢ Biswal, Arati. (2003). "The Emergent Feminine Psyche in Indian Women Novelists Writing in English." Re-Markings. 1.2: 59-66.
➢ Friedan, Betty. (1984). The Feminine Mystique. Canada: Penguin Books.

- Greer, Germain. (1999). The Whole Woman. London: Doubleday.
- Grimke, Sarah. (1837). Letters on the Equality of the Sexes. 27 July. <http://www.pinn.net/~sunshine/book-sum/grimke3.html>
- Nayar, Pramod K. (2002). Literary Theory Today. New Delhi: Asia Book Club.
- Russell, Bertrand. (1929). Marriage and Morals. Canada: Bantuin Publishers.
- Ruth, Sheila. (1995). Issues in Feminism: An Introduction to Women Studies (third edition). California: Mayfield Publishing Company.
- De, Shobhaa. (1989). Socialite Evenings. New Delhi: Penguin Books.
- - - - . (1991). Starry Nights. New Delhi: Penguin Books.
- - - - . (1992). Sisters. New Delhi: Penguin Books.
- - - - . (1992). Strange Obsession. New Delhi: Penguin Books.
- Vakil, Ashwina. (2003). "'I don't have to please anybody so I don't suck up to anybody.'" Rediff On The Net: Shobha De discusses her latest bestseller. 7 November. <http://www.rediff.com/news/feb/12shobh2.htm>.
- Woolf, Virginia. (1996). A Room of One's Own. London: Vintage.

CHAPTER-8

Some Home Truths of Being LGBTQ

-Anoushka Tyagi
anushenuu@gmail.com

Although homosexuality and strange personalities are now acceptable to a greater number of Indian adolescents than at any other time in history, acknowledgment of their sexuality and the ability to openly communicate their sex decisions remain a constant battle for LGBT (lesbian, gay, sexually open, transsexual) people within the confines of their families, homes, and schools. In metropolitan India, where web-based media and corporate campaigns have increased public awareness of LGBT rights, the situation appears to be better for homosexual men than for transsexuals or lesbian women. While urban LGBT voices heard on a few online and real-world stages form a substantial part of LGBT advocacy, they just scratch the surface of the various challenges faced by the local LGBT community.

Families in rural India have their own unique ways of dealing with LGBT individuals, far from gay pride marches, meet-ups, and pleasant Twitter exchanges. Secret honour killings are common in some areas, so the only option for a young gay guy to survive is to depart in the middle of the night to a city with little money or social support. Lesbian women in several regions of the world are subjected to family-sanctioned therapeutic assaults, which are regularly carried out by their own relatives. Lesbian women and transmen in rural areas, according to Vyjayanti Vasanta Mogli, a transwoman LGBT advocate and public arrangement researcher at Tata Institute of Social Sciences in Hyderabad, who has openly spoken about her mistreatment at school, end up at the bottom.

When criticising the country's financial situation, she invokes B.R. Ambedkar. "Ambedkar regarded the town to be a unit of viciousness," she says, adding that this is also true for LGBT concerns. "Lesbians are routinely assaulted by town surgeons and babas in order to rid them of their homosexuality. Refusing to marry leads to more physical abuse. Family recognition stories that you see on TV and in other media are more of a metropolitan oddity." Suicides by lesbian women are frequent and noteworthy, even in educated metropolitan India. It should come as no surprise, then, that a court recently concluded that lesbians in India face the greatest danger from their own families.

The following are the outcomes of the investigation:

One of the fundamental points that results in the slander of LGBT people, according to a new report, is parental response to homosexuality. The assessment goes on to say that most LGBT people are fine with their families as long as they agree to act like heteros. Sovereign Manvendra Singh Gohil, whose storey of coming out has been widely publicised in recent years, now leads a number of initiatives to aid LGBT persons, including the Lakshya Trust, which works to combat HIV/AIDS in the LGBT community. He claims that people who identify as LGBT should not be swept up by what they see in the media. "I was in the storeroom for a reason, and it was no small one.", he also declares "I know of someone who received an unexpected burst of motivation from a television show and chose to come out to his family." It was a complete failure. He had lost everything: his home, his job, and his possessions. I usually encourage people to be completely aware of their surroundings. Be financially prepared. Before you take this step, segregate a bit of yourself from your family, both emotionally and financially. Mr Gay India 2016, Anwesh Sahoo, who came out to his family when he was 16 years old, has a different perspective: "I would not advocate waiting for the perfect time." Remaining in the closet is a huge mental burden. Assuming you and your family approach data, I advise you to do so at any time.

Nonetheless, Mogli warns about the widespread practise of family pressuring LGBT people to undergo "remedial" treatment. She had to spend a lengthy time in a mental institution once she was released.

Her deep scepticism of the medical field has also been exacerbated by the event. "I was treated like a crook in the mental ward, which resembled a jail replete with high dividers and an electrified border," she recalls. "I was put on crazy drugs, which caused me to be sad and disorganised. The specialist subjected me to torturous psychosexual trials by forcing me to stay with other insane women. She wanted to know how I reacted to their cooperation and vulgar gestures. This similar person has now adjusted her training to make it easier.

I'm not implying that all professionals are dishonest, but LGBT people and their families should be aware that some professionals explore directions just to shift their current practises to something that will bring them more customers and money. Sakshi Juneja, the founder of Gaysi, an online community for LGBT people, believes that there is never enough design. " You owe no one anything if you don't come out. In this case, I would advise you to take as much time as you need and limit yourself to only those with whom you are comfortable. Prior to speaking with your family, monetary and emotional dependability are unmistakable requirements. By the end of the day, your relatives only want you to have a safe future, therefore it helps if you don't turn.

"Parmesh Shahani, the chairman of Godrej India Culture Lab and the author of Gay Bombay, hasn't the foggiest clue of a single person whose life turned out to be more dreadful in the long run as a result of being out." Despite the fact that it is a test, I am a firm believer in people coming out. I'm aware of several families who have grown closer as a result of someone's decision to come out. I'd recommend enlisting the assistance of a good asset group and, if feasible, an LGBT-friendly guide. When you come out, all you're doing is letting others know who you are. You're not seeking their approval or acknowledgement. Allow them the time they require to process, and ask questions.

"Parmesh Shahani, the chairman of Godrej India Culture Lab and the author of Gay Bombay, hasn't the foggiest clue of a single person whose life turned out to be more dreadful in the long run as a result of being out." Despite the fact that it is a test, I am a firm believer in people coming out. I'm aware of several families who have grown closer as a result of someone's decision to come out. I'd recommend enlisting the assistance of a good asset group and, if feasible, an LGBT-friendly guide. When you come out, all you're doing is letting others know who you are. You're not seeking their approval or acknowledgement. Allow them the time they require to process, and ask questions.

Juneja was inspired to start Gaysi because she felt there was a need for a space where LGBT people could discuss their experiences. "I needed to provide a platform for us to interact and share our biographies. When I first started Gaysi, there were few avenues for lesbian women to collaborate and communicate with one another." The absence of parental assistance may be weakening, but that does not imply the sky has fallen, according to Shahani. " I know a lot of LGBT people who have formed elective care groups, or family-like groupings, when their own families haven't been stable. Fortunately, we have strong LGBT affiliations and networks in most large urban neighbourhoods in metropolitan India, so individuals are not alone", as well as he exclaims, In any case, access to secure online places and support groups rarely compensates for the void left by family opposition. According to Gohil, many LGBT people succumb to the pressure to marry despite the lack of family support. "Many lesbian women approach me with requests to witness a gay man who might be willing to put up with this marriage display. They won't have to worry about coming out or sexual abuse, and they'll be able to meet their family's marriage requirement." According to Shahani, any parent's first responsibility is to recognise and respect their children's individuality. "Tolerance does not assist your child. You're just doing your job. By tolerating your child, you are also contributing to a better society that values diversity and recognises people for who they are "he declares "An eccentric person has multiple struggles in all aspects of life," Jyoti explains. "If guardians don't add to these disputes, they can make their children's lives much easier. The basic issue is that parents have a hard time accepting their children as sexual beings. Any discussion of sexuality and sexual or sex character is hindered and encircled by shame in this way. This is the point at which responsibility and chaos begin. When children ask awkward questions, most guardians try to keep them quiet. Guardians must discover out how to tune in and allow others to do so.

Famous TV shows, for example, Satyamev Jayate and The Tara Sharma Show have helped bring issues to light among guardians about LGBT issues. Jyoti says a portion of his companions essentially requested that their folks watch the episode of Satyamev Jayate that zeroed in on substitute sexualities as opposed to attempting to clarify everything all alone. Sahoo says TV helped him through days when he was too youthful to even think about seeing all that he went through. Without a trace of open correspondence with his family, his good examples included characters from Modern Family and entertainer Jim Parsons (who plays Sheldon Cooper in The Big Bang Theory). He adds that TV has the greatest arrive at with regards to impacting both the senior and more youthful ages.

Here I would like to quote the example of Christine Jorgensen (May 30, 1926 – May 3, 1989) .She was the United States' first well-known transsexual woman. Jorgensen was born and raised in the Bronx, New York City. She was drafted into the United States Army shortly after graduating from high school in 1945 during World War II. She went to a variety of schools and worked following her army duty. At this time, she was introduced to gender reassignment surgery. Jorgensen travelled around Europe and was awarded a unique licence to work on a series of projects that began in 1952 in Copenhagen, Denmark. She returned to the United States in the early 1950s, and the New York Times covered her reintegration on the front page.

She became well-known as a result of her fast rise to prominence. She was also noted for her candour and sophisticated wit, and she utilised her position to advocate for transgender people. She was also an actress and a nightclub performer, as well as a singer who recorded many songs. Jorgensen delivered several speeches about his transgender experience, and in 1967 he published an autobiography. Jorgensen graduated from Christopher Columbus High School in

1945 and was drafted into the United States Army at the age of 19 years old. After being discharged from the Army, she attended Mohawk Valley Community College in Utica, New York, the Progressive School of Photography in New Haven, Connecticut, and the Manhattan Medical and Dental Assistant School in New York City. She also did some work for Pathé News for a while. Christine Jorgensen became aware of sex reassignment surgery after hearing about it from a friend after returning to New York after serving in the military and becoming increasingly concerned about a "lack of manly physical development," as one obituary put it later. She started taking oestrogen in the form of ethinylestradio and began researching the surgery after receiving advise from Joseph Angelo, the husband of a student at the Manhattan Medical and Dental Assistant School. Jorgensen intended to travel to Sweden, where the treatment would be performed by the only doctors in the world at the time. During a visit to meet relatives in Copenhagen, she met Christian Hamburger, a Danish endocrinologist and specialist in rehabilitative hormonal therapy. Jorgensen stayed in Denmark and underwent hormone replacement therapy. Jorgensen stayed in Denmark and under Hamburger's supervision received hormone replacement therapy. She chose the name Christine in honour of Hamburger.

Her special permission was given by the Danish Minister of Justice. On September 24, 1951, Jorgensen had an orchiectomy at Gentofte Hospital in Copenhagen. She wrote a letter to friends on October 8, 1951, detailing how the surgery had affected her.

The other modifications, on the other hand, are significantly more substantial. Do you remember the shy, miserable person who fled America? That person is no longer present, and everyone saw she was in good spirits.

In November 1952, doctors at Copenhagen University Hospital performed a penectomy. "My second procedure, like the first, was not as major a process as it appears," Jorgensen explains. She later returned to the United States and underwent a vaginoplasty when the treatment became available. Angelo oversaw the vaginoplasty, which was done with the help of medical advisor Harry Benjamin.

Harry Benjamin praised her with boosting Jorgensen's studies in the prologue to his memoirs. "Indeed, Christine, none of this would have happened if it hadn't been for you; the prize, my papers, lectures, and so on," he wrote.

The New York Daily News published a front-page storey titled "Ex-GI Becomes Blonde Beauty" on December 1, 1952, asserting (incorrectly) that Jorgensen was the first person to have a "sex change." In the late 1920s and early 1930s, German physicians performed this type of surgery. Magnus Hirschfeld treated Dorchen Richter and Lili Elbe, a Danish artist, at the same time. Dorchen Richter and Lili Elbe, a Danish artist, were both notable recipients of similar surgeries and were both patients of Magnus Hirschfeld at the Institut für Sexualwissenschaft in Berlin.

Following her transition and gender reassignment surgery, she received a lot of attention "For decades, she has served as a role model for other transsexuals. Ms. Jorgensen's poise, charm, and wit won the hearts of millions. She was a tireless lecturer on the subject of transsexuality, pleading for understanding from a public that all too often wanted to see transsexuals as freaks or perverts..." However, as time passed, the press became less enamoured with her and began to analyse her more closely. She was frequently requested by the print media if she would pose naked for them. Jorgensen wanted to marry labour union statistician John Traub after her vaginoplasty, but the engagement was called off. In Massapequa Park, New York, where her father had built her a mansion after her reassignment surgery, she announced her engagement to typewriter Howard J. Knox in 1959. She and Knox married and became members of a Lutheran church. However, because Jorgensen's birth certificate classified her as a male, the pair was unable to acquire a marriage licence. The New York Times reported in a storey about the broken engagement that Knox had lost his job in Washington, D.C. after his engagement to Jorgensen was revealed. Jorgensen came to California in 1967 after her parents died. For a time, she abandoned the ranch house built by her father in Massapequa and stayed in the Chateau Marmont in Los Angeles. Jorgensen's autobiography, Christine Jorgensen: A Personal Autobiography, was published the same year, chronicling her life experiences as a transsexual and including her own personal thoughts on important events in her life. During the 1970s and 1980s, Jorgensen spoke about her experiences on university campuses and other settings. Her directness and sophisticated wit were well-known. When Vice President Spiro T. Agnew referred to Charles Goodell as "the Christine Jorgensen of the Republican Party," she sought an apology from him. Her request was turned down by Agnew.

Jorgensen has worked as an actress and a nightclub performer, and he has a number of songs to his credit. She played Madame Rosepettle in the summer stock productions of Oh Dad, Poor Dad, Mamma's Hung You in the Closet, and I'm Feelin' So Sad. She sang several songs in her nightclub act, including "I Enjoy Being a Girl," during which she changed into a Wonder Woman costume at the conclusion. Warner Communications, the copyright owners of the Wonder Woman character, asked that she stop using the character, which she did and replaced with a new character of her own creation, Superwoman, who was distinguished by a giant letter S on her cape. Jorgensen continued her performance until at least 1982, when she performed twice in the Hollywood area: once at the Backlot Theatre, near to the discothèque Studio One, and again at The Frog Pond restaurant. This performance was recorded and is now available on iTunes as an album. Jorgensen returned to Copenhagen in 1984 to perform her show, and was included in the Danish transgender documentary film Paradiset er ikke til salg, directed by Teit Ritzau (Paradise Is Not for Sale). Jorgensen was the first and only known trans woman to perform at Oscar's Delmonico Restaurant in Manhattan, which drew criticism from the restaurant's proprietors, Oscar and Mario Tucci.

So, I believe, the sooner the better. Because you have to face the world off whenever you come out of the closet. If God has made you special, He knows you have the courage to fight and establish your identity.

Do not spend your valuable life in darkness. Come out and embrace the Rainbow with pride!

References

➢ Jorgensen, Christine (1968). *Christine Jorgensen: a personal autobiography*. New York: Bantam. p. 8. OCLC 1023834324

➢ *"21 Transgender People Who Influenced American Culture". Time.*

➢ *^ Docter, Richard F. (February 2013). Becoming a Woman: A Biography of Christine Jorgensen. ISBN 9781136576355.*

➢ *^ Jorgensen, Christine (1968). Christine Jorgensen: a personal autobiography. New York: Bantam. p. 8. OCLC 1023834324.*

➢ *^ Ingrassia, Michelle (May 5, 1989). "Transsexual Superstar: In 1952, She Was a Scandal: When Jorgensen decided to change his name—and his body—the nation wasn't quite ready". Newsday. p. A1.*

➢ *^ "Education: Students Wanted". Time. September 2, 1946. Archived from the original on February 20, 2009. Retrieved April 30, 2010.*

➢ *^ Jump up to:ᵃ ᵇ ᶜ Bullough, Vern L. "Jorgensen, Christine (30 May 1926 – 3 May 1989)". Archived from the original on February 22, 2009.*

➢ *^ Zimmerman, Jonathan. "Caitlyn Jenner, meet Christine Jorgensen". NY Daily News. Retrieved July 27, 2017.*

➢ *^ Meyerowitz, Joanne J. (June 30, 2009). How Sex Changed. Harvard University Press. pp. 19–21. ISBN 978-0-674-04096-0.*

➢ *^ Jump up to:ᵃ ᵇ Kelly, Erin (June 2, 2015). "Call Her Christine: The Original American Trans Celebrity". All That's Interesting, 2. Retrieved September 17, 2020.*

➢ *^ Whittle, Stephen (June 2, 2010). "A brief history of transgender issues". The Guardian. Retrieved August 22, 2019.*

CHAPTER-9

LGBT

(Their History, Policies, Amendments and Literature)

-Yashi Bansal

yashibansal1995@gmail.com

This chapter aims to bring out the detrimental condition of our so-called modern society. We always try to fit in the shoes of foreigners but We Never Can, not at least for the next 10-15 more years. There have been many "prathas" and beliefs like sati pratha, tradition of dahej, honor killing, child labour, feticide and many more that existed and still exists in our society to worsen the condition. Having belonged to LGBT community is such a same taboo in our society. LGBT is an acronym that stands for the Lesbian, Gay, Bisexual, and Transgender community which has always faced the bad side of our social society. People who belong to this community have love or affectionate interest in people of the same sex or both (same and opposite).

The author will talk about the adverse conditions of the people of the said community, how the situations have changed or remained same in the modern era. This chapter will throw some light on the history of the community along with the new norms which have been formed for them. Also, the liberties given to them, by the Indian Government. With this theme in mind, the chapter will also include some examples of how these people are portrayed and talked about in literature and how writers belonging to this community were and are criticized or celebrated.

According to historian and philosopher Michel Foucault, homosexual and heterosexual identities did not emerge until the nineteenth century. Prior to that, he explained, the labels were used to define activities rather than identities. The birth date of sexual orientation classification, according to Foucault, was Karl Westphal's renowned 1870 article Contrary Sexual Feeling. Some researchers, on the other hand, suggest that there are considerable parallels between previous and modern conceptions of sexuality, citing the use of multiple words for homosexuality. (*Terminology of homosexuality*)

Plato, the ancient Greek logician, pictured (through the persona of the profane joke artist Aristophanes) three sexual directions - heterosexuality, male homosexuality, and female homosexuality - and offered explanations for their reality using a made-up creation legend in his Symposium.

Certain groups have adopted the term trans as a more inclusive alternative to "transsexual," where trans (without the reference mark) has been used to portray trans men and trans ladies, whereas trans encompasses all non-cisgender (genderqueer) characters, including transsexual, transgender, cross dresser, genderqueer, genderfluid, non-paired, genderfuck, genderless, agender, non-gendered, third sexual orientation, two-soul persona. Similarly, the term transgender is commonly grouped with the term transsexual, but some transgender people object to this. When transsexual people are not included, the more limited term LGB is used instead of LGBT.

There are numerous variations, even those that change the request for the letters; LGBT or GLBT are the most often used terms. Despite their similar importance, LGBT may have a more feminist undertone than GLBT because it places the "L" (for "lesbian") first. LGBT may also include extra Qs for "eccentric" or "addressing." LGBT slang was first used by activist groups in the United States in 1988. Until the 1990s, gay, lesbian, bisexual, and transgender people were not treated fairly within the movement. As a result, in 1999, some entities, such as the GLBT Historical Society, changed their names. While there has been much debate in the LGBT community about the public adoption of various individuals and groups (bisexual and transgender people, in particular, have been shunned by the larger LGBT community), the term LGBT has served as a good symbol of inclusivity.

History and instances of treatment of people for having different choices:
(Bonnie J. Morris, PhD)

Notwithstanding, all through 150 years of gay social developments (generally from the 1870s to now), pioneers and coordinators battled to address the altogether different concerns and character issues of gay men, ladies distinguishing as lesbians, and others recognizing as sex variation or nonbinary. White, male and Western activists whose gatherings and hypotheses acquired influence against homophobia didn't really address the scope of racial, class and public characters confounding a more extensive LGBT plan. Ladies were frequently left out through and through.

What is the pre-history of LGBT activism?
Most historians agree that there is substantiation of gay movement and same-sex love in every documented culture, regardless of whether such connections were acknowledged or oppressed. We understand that homosexuality existed in ancient Israel chiefly as it is disallowed in the Bible, despite the fact that it flourished between all types of people in Ancient Greece. Considerable body of evidence for people who spent the entire lives as a people with a different sexual orientation than they were identified when they were born.

What may have been discovered regarding same-sex love or sexual orientation personality was covered in embarrassment against the emerging panorama of public power and Christian confidence. In fact, both the armed conflict between emerging countries and the takeoff of male warriors abandoned ladies to live and created solid connections amongst males as well. Where it was frowned upon for unmarried, irrelevant males and females to mix or interact openly, same-sex friendship developed. Ladies' connections were exempt from scrutiny because there was no risk of pregnancy. Regardless, across a large part of the world, female sexual mobility and feeling were restricted since genital circumcision practices made clitoridectomy a permanent norm. Ladies and young ladies, financially abused by the sexism which kept them from occupations and monetary/instruction openings assigned for men just, might pass as male to access desired encounters or pay. This was a decision made by numerous ladies who were not really transsexual in character. Ladies "camouflaged" themselves as men, now and then for expanded times of years, to battle in the armed services (Deborah Sampson) to act as a privateer (Mary Read and Anne Bonney), go to clinical school, and so on All kinds of people who lived as an alternate sex were regularly just found after their demises, as the outrageous contrasts in male versus female apparel and prepping in quite a bit of Western culture made "passing" shockingly simple in specific conditions.

Additionally, jobs in artistic expressions where ladies were prohibited from working necessitated that men be selected to assume female parts, frequently making a high-status, serious market for those we may today recognize as transwomen, in settings from Shakespeare's auditorium to Japanese Kabuki to the Chinese show. This acknowledgment of execution specialists, and the fame of "drag" humor diversely, didn't really check the beginning of transsexual promotion, however made human expressions a frequently tolerating asylum for LGBT people who fabricated dramatic vocations based around camouflage and dream.

Sigmund Freud, writing in a similar time, didn't think about homosexuality as an ailment or a wrongdoing and accepted sexual openness to be a natural angle starting with dubious sex advancement in the belly. However, Freud likewise felt that lesbian cravings were a youthfulness ladies could defeat through hetero marriage and male predominance. These works continuously streamed down to an inquisitive public through magazines and introductions, arriving at people frantic to more deeply study those such as themselves, including some like English essayist Radclyffe Hall who eagerly acknowledged being a "innate rearrange."

Until after World War II, there were little efforts in the United States to create marketing groups fostering homosexual and lesbian ties. In any event, prewar homosexual life thrived in metropolitan areas such as New York's Greenwich Village and Harlem during the 1920s Harlem Renaissance. The blues music of African-American ladies exhibited assortments of lesbian longing, battle and humor; these exhibitions, alongside male and female drag stars, acquainted a gay hidden world with straight supporters during Prohibition's insubordination of race and sex codes in speakeasy clubs. The disturbances of World War II permitted in the past confined gay people to meet as fighters and war laborers; and different volunteers were removed from unassuming communities and posted around the world.

The Mattachine Society, founded in 1950 by Harry Hay and Chuck Rowland, was the coordinating body for homosexual men as an oppressed social minority. Other notable homophile organization on the West Coast were One, Inc., which was founded in 1952, and Daughters of Bilitis, which was founded in 1955 by Phyllis Lyon and Del Martin. These meetings provided data and effort to thousands of people through gatherings and distributes. These early associations soon discovered assistance from prominent sociologists and therapists.

Stall is still seen as a watershed moment in homosexual pride, and it has been commemorated since the 1970s with "satisfaction walks" conducted each June around the United States. Ongoing grants have called for more recognition of the roles that drag entertainers, minorities, bisexuals, and transsexual supporters played in the Stonewall Riots. The gay freedom development of the 1970s saw bunch political associations spring up, frequently at chances with each other. Disappointed with the male authority of most gay freedom gatherings, lesbians affected by the women's activist development of the 1970s shaped its own gatherings, record labels, live performances, publications, book stores, and distribution companies, and advocated for lesbian rights in traditional women's activist gatherings such as the National Organization for Women (NOW).

Social occasions, for example, ladies' music shows, book shop readings and lesbian celebrations past the United States were phenomenally effective in getting sorted out ladies to become activists; the women's activist development against aggressive behavior at home likewise helped ladies to leave oppressive relationships, while holding guardianship of kids turned into a principal issue for lesbian moms.

The United Church of Christ named the first openly homosexual pastor in 1972, as the church's rigorous acceptance of LGBT persons grew. Soon after, more gay and lesbian church and temple events followed. The Guardians and Friends of Lesbians and Gays (PFLAG), founded in 1972, provided relatives with more prominent support positions in the growth of LGBT rights.

VIP artists, both homosexual and straight, remained among the most vociferous advocates advocating for resilience and equal rights. With increased media consideration for gay and lesbian social equality in the 1990s, trans and intersex voices began to gain space through works such as Kate Boernstein's "Sexual orientation Outlaw" (1994) and "My Gender Workbook" (1998), Ann Fausto-"Fantasies Sterling's of Gender" (1992), and Leslie Feinberg's Transgender Warriors (1998), upgrading shifts in ladies' and sex studies to become more comprehensive of trans. Because to the relentless efforts of several groups and individuals, aided by web and post office-based postal crusade organizing, the twenty-first century heralded new legal rights for gay and lesbian couples. In 2000, Vermont law considers same-sex common associations, and Massachusetts became the first state to perform same-sex couples in 2004; with the repeal of state homosexuality laws (Lawrence v. Texas, 2003), gay and lesbian Americans were finally emancipated from criminal classification.

Homosexual marriage was initially legalized in the Netherlands, Belgium, Spain, and Canada; nevertheless, the acceptance of gay marriage by church and state has continued to divide opinion across the world. Following the tremendous advancements for LGBT liberties in post-politically sanctioned racial segregation South Africa, moderate evangelicals in the United States began donating assistance and funding for homophobic missions abroad. Uganda's spectacular death penalty for homosexuals and lesbians was maybe the most severe in Africa.The first decade of the twenty-first century saw a renewed emphasis on transgender activism and an increase in the use of terminology that addressed paired sex differentiating evidence. Images of trans women appeared increasingly often in cinema and television, as did programmes featuring same-sex couples raising children.

Transphobia, cissexism, and other vocabulary (for example, "hir" and "them") became accepted, and film and television programming included more openly trans kids and adults. However, tensions among lesbian and trans activists remained, with the long-running Michigan Womyn's Music Festival boycotted by many LGBT groups over the subject of trans consideration. Michfest, like other lady-only occasions with a substantially lesbian foundation, has sustained an ideal of gathering ladies and young ladies conceived feminine. The memorial came to an end in August 2015, following its 40th anniversary.

Web activism expanded, while a considerable lot of people in general, actual social occasion spaces that once characterized LGBT activism (bars, book shops, ladies' live events) started to disappear, and the use of "eccentric" swapped lesbian distinguishing proof for some more youthful ladies activists. Consideration moved to worldwide activism as U.S. gains were not coordinated by comparable equivalent privileges laws in the 75 different nations where homosexuality stayed unlawful.

Starting at 2016, LGBT ID and activism was as yet deserving of death in ten nations: Iran, Iraq, Mauritania, Nigeria, Qatar, Saudi Arabia, Somalia, Sudan, Uganda and Yemen; the predicament of the LGBT people group in Russia got extreme concentration during the 2014 Winter Olympic Games, to which President Obama sent an unexpected of out LGBT competitors. Strong comments from the new Pope Francis ("Who am I to pass judgment?") offered desire to LGBT Catholics around the world. Maybe the best changes in the U.S. happened between spring 2015 and spring 2016: in pre-summer 2015 Alison Bechdel's lesbian-themed Broadway creation Fun Home won a few Tony grants, previous Olympic hero Bruce Jenner changed to Caitlyn Jenner, and afterward in June of 2015, the Supreme Court choice perceived same-sex marriage (Obergefell v. Hodges).

The probable suppression of personality that may have played a role in the executioner's choice of victim has raised increased awareness of the cost of homophobia – hidden or socially conveyed – in and outside the United States. A truly inclusive society remains an elusive goal for the Indian LGBT community. Last year, LGBT campaigners in India won when the Supreme Court consistently overturned Section 377 of India's penal code, which criminalized same-sex relationships. Equity Indu Malhotra said unequivocally that "a conciliatory emotion [is owed] to members from the LGBT people group... for the ostracism and cruelty they faced as a result of society's obliviousness." In 2014, the Supreme Court issued a broad ruling in NALSA v. India, holding that transsexual persons should be lawfully perceived by their sex character, have access to all essential rights, and benefit from extraordinary benefits in education and business.

In any event, while legal reforms are an important step, much more is necessary for LGBT people in India to have the opportunity to live without division and with dignity. Children who are bullied at school are less likely to prosper and are more likely to perceive themselves as vulnerable against separation and viciousness as adults.

Basic liberties Watch research in different settings across the world whether in South Africa, Kenya, Jamaica, or the US shows that weakness as grown-ups associates with negative encounters as youngsters whether at home or in school. Moving India to being a country that secures sexual and sex variety will require activity by numerous services and offices at both the public and state levels. This incorporates altering instruction laws to incorporate a range of sex – not simply "male and female" understudies – and refreshing educational programs to make them comprehensive of different sex and sexuality networks so all understudies are getting precise data. Most students of history concur that there is proof of gay movement and same-sex love, regardless of whether such connections were acknowledged or abused, in each recorded culture. (*history-young-lgbt-indians-need-concrete-policies-protect-them-bullying*)

The Early Gay Rights Movement in Other countries and India:

In 1924, Henry Gerber, a German immigrant, founded the Society for Human Rights in Chicago, which became the most well-known homosexual rights organization in the United States. During his leadership of the United States Armed Forces in World War I, Gerber was inspired to join the Scientific-Humanitarian Committee, a "gay liberation" group in Germany.

For the next several years, the growth of homosexual rights declined, although LGBT individuals all over the world came into the limelight a handful of times. For example, when she released her lesbian-themed novel, The Well of Loneliness, in 1928, English artist and creator Radclyffe Hall sparked debate. Furthermore, during World War II, the Nazis imprisoned homosexual individuals in horrific conditions, branding them with the infamous pink triangle identity, which was also given to sexual stalkers.

In addition, Alfred Kinsey proposed in his 1948 book Sexual Behavior in the Human Male that male sexual orientation exists on a spectrum ranging from entirely homosexual to solely hetero.

Harry Hay founded the Mattachine Foundation, one of the country's first LGBT rights organizations, in 1950. The Los Angeles association gave rise to the term "homophile," which was perceived as less clinical and more focused on sexual activity than "gay." Nonetheless, the establishment, which attempted to work on the lives of gay men through conversation gatherings and similar exercises, expanded after founding component Dale Jennings was arrested in 1952 for sales and then let free because of a paused jury. Toward the end of the year, Jennings formed another initiative called One, Inc., which invited females and distributed ONE, the country's first gay-friendly magazine. Jennings was fired from One, Inc. in 1953 for being a socialist—he and Harry Hay were both fired from the Mattachine Foundation for their socialism—yet the journal continued. That same year, four lesbian couples in San Francisco formed the Daughters of Bilitis, who soon began distributing a brochure called The Ladder, the major lesbian distribution of any kind.

During the 1970s, LGBT people's emergence and activism aided the growth on a variety of fronts. For example, the New York Supreme Court ruled in 1977 that transgender lady Renée Richards may compete in the US Open tennis tournament as a lady.

In addition, a few openly LGBT persons have been elected to public office: Kathy Kozachenko was elected to the Ann Harbor, Michigan, City Council in 1974, becoming the first openly gay American elected to public office. Harvey Milk, who campaigned on a pro-gay-liberties platform, was elected mayor of San Francisco in 1978, becoming the state's first openly homosexual politician. The District of Columbia approved a rule in 1992 that allowed homosexual and lesbian couples to register as domestic accomplices, granting them some of the liberties of marriage (the city of San Francisco passed a comparable law three years earlier and California would later stretch out those privileges to the whole state in 1999). The highest court in Hawaii ruled in 1993 that a ban on homosexual marriage would violate the state constitution. Regardless, state residents objected, and in 1998, a law forbidding marriage of the same sexes.

In 2003, gay rights activists received additional good news when the United States Supreme Court, in Lawrence v. Texas, overturned the state's anti-homosexuality legislation. The landmark decision fully decriminalized homosexual relationships across the country. In 2015, the Supreme Court ruled that states could not prohibit same-sex marriage, rendering sure it stays that way throughout the country.

The United States military repealed its ban on transgender people serving openly in 2016, a month after Eric Fanning became Secretary of the Army and the first out homosexual secretary of a U.S. military service. President Donald Trump announced another transgender strategy for the tactical in March 2018, which once again barred most transsexual persons from military assistance. President Biden signed a leader request to end the embargo on January 25, 2021, his sixth day in office.

On August 24, 2017, India's Supreme Court granted the country's LGBT community the right to safely express their sexual orientation. As a result, a person's sexual orientation is protected by the country's Right to Privacy statute. However, the Supreme Court did not overturn any statutes prohibiting same-sex unions outright.

The Supreme Court of India approved consented homosexual sex on September 6, 2018. Segment 377 of the Indian Penal Code (IPC), which dates back to 1861, declares sexual acts "against the request of nature" to be unlawful and punishable by death. On December 2002, the Naz Foundation filed a Public Interest Litigation (PIL) in the Delhi High Court to challenge IPC Section 377. On July 4, 2008, the Delhi High Court observed "the same old thing" in hosting a gay convention, which is customary outside of India.

On 2nd July 2009, on account of Naz Foundation v National Capital Territory of Delhi, the High Court of Delhi struck down a lot of S. 377 of the IPC as being illegal. The Court held that to the degree. 377 condemned consensual non-vaginal sexual demonstrations between grown-ups, it abused a singular's major privileges to correspondence under the watchful eye of the law, independence from segregation and to life and individual freedom under Articles 14, 15 and 21 of the Constitution of India. The High Court didn't strike down Section 377 totally. It held the segment to be substantial in the event of non-consensual non-vaginal intercourse or to intercourse with minors, and it communicated the expectation that Parliament would authoritatively address the issue.

The following is the decision of the Delhi High Court:

"We declare that Section 377 of the IPC, inasmuch as it outlaws consensual sexual demonstrations by adults in private, violates Articles 21, 14, and 15 of the Constitution. Section 377 of the IPC will continue to govern non-consensual penile non-vaginal intercourse and penile non-vaginal sex with children. Furthermore, we stress that our decision will not result in the re-opening of criminal matters, including those under Section 377 of the IPC, that have already been closed and finality was successfully attained. On 28 January 2014, Supreme Court excused the audit request documented by Central Government, Naz Foundation and a few others, against its 11 December decision on Section 377 of IPC. In January 2015, National Crime Records Bureau (NCRB) said that as indicated by information gathered, 778 cases were documented under Section 377 of IPC and 587 captures were made in 2014 until October after the Supreme Court decision. A few states are yet to present their full data. On December 18, 2015, Shashi Tharoor, an Indian National Congress member, introduced a Private Members Bill in the Lok Sabha to legalize Section 377 of the Indian Penal Code; however, the bill was defeated by a vote of 71–24 with one abstention. On March 12, 2016, Tharoor introduced a Private Members Bill to decriminalize Section 377. Nonetheless, the presenting movement was defeated once more by a vote of 58–14, with one abstention. On February 2, 2016, the Supreme Court agreed to reconsider its 2013 decision; it stated that it would refer applications to repeal Section 377 to a five-part created seat, which would result in a far-reaching becoming aware of the matter. On August 24, 2016, the Union Cabinet approved a draught law for a boycott of corporate surrogacy, which was revealed by Sushma Swaraj, the Minister of External Affairs (India). The draught bill barred homosexual persons from having proxy children, with Swaraj stating, "We don't consider live-in and gay ties as being against our culture." On 24 August 2017, the Supreme Court maintained that the right to individual protection is an "inherent" and principal directly under the constitution. In its 547-page choice on security freedoms, the nine-judge seat likewise held that "sexual direction is a fundamental trait of protection". The judgment noted, "Victimization a person based on sexual direction is profoundly hostile to the nobility and self-esteem of the person. Correspondence requests that the sexual direction of every person in the public eye should be secured on an even stage. The right to security and the assurance of sexual direction lie at the center of the basic freedoms ensured by Articles 14, 15 and 21 of the Constitution." On 10 July 2018, the Supreme Court maintained the significance of the freedoms of the LGBT people group. Equity D. Y. Chandrachud, in the procedures of the court, held that picking an accomplice was each individual's central right. On September 6, 2018, the Supreme Court overturned a portion of Section 377, a British-period regulation that condemned consenting homosexual activities. The court stated that some sections of Area 377 prohibiting unnatural intercourse with children and animals will remain in effect. On July 29, 2012, Anjali Gopalan started the city's first LGBTQ Rainbow celebration and kicked off Asia's first Gender eccentric pride march as part of the Turing Rainbow festival coordinated by Srishti Madurai, an abstract and asset circle for elective sex and sexualities. It was founded by Gopi Shankar, a student at The American College in Madurai, to eliminate social segregation faced by the LGBT and Genderfluid communities. The association's goal is to showcase 20 different types of Genders.

Surat hosted the main LGBT pride march in Gujarat state on October 6, 2013. Rajasthan's first pride event occurred on March 1, 2015, when a pride walk was organized in Jaipur. Sushant Divgikar, the 2014 Mr. Gay India winner, was a contestant on the Bigg Boss reality program. The sixth All-Kerala Queer Pride Parade was held in Kochi on July 26, 2014. It was organized by Queerala (a support group for LGBT persons) and Sahayathrika (a rights association for lesbian and sexually unbiased ladies in Kerala). In June 2016, a stage called Amour Queer Dating was launched in India to enable eccentric/LGBTIQ persons find long haul relationships.

Reference and Treatment in Literature:

The ancient Indian classic Kamasutra, authored by Vtsyyana, devotes an entire chapter to sensual gay behaviour.In Shyam Selvadurai's "Funny Boy," the protagonist, Arjie, is a gay man who is constantly subjected to stereotypes he does not wish to follow. As soon as Jegan enters the novel, he befriends Arjie, and for the first time, Arjie's gay impulses float to the forefront, as Arjie admires "how built he was, the way his thighs crushed against his jeans." The novel's first portion begins with the grandkids gathering at Ammachi and Appachi's house for the spend-the-days. Arjie and his female relatives play "bride-bride," as is usual, until Tanuja (Her Fatness) refuses to fulfil Arjie's yearning to be a bride. When the adults discover out what they're up to, one uncle tells Arjie's father, "You've got a crazy one here." Arjie is no longer allowed to interact with the women. When he queries his mother, she replies, "Because the sky is so high and pigs can't fly."

The Arthashastra, an Indian book on statecraft written in the second century BCE, lists a wide range of sexual acts that, whether conducted with a man or a woman, were intended to be penalized with the lowest degree of fine. Whereas gay intercourse was not sanctioned, it was considered a minor offence, while certain types of heterosexual intercourse were penalized more harshly.

The Color Purple by Alice Walker is not a novel about homosexuality, although it does include some of its hues. Alice Walker left no room for doubt regarding Celie and Shug Avery's courtship. There is love, sensitivity, and caring between these two characters, which stands out even more in light of the fact that this book is situated in a world where Black women are frequently denied all three. There is also passion. Celie and Shug's connection is very sexual: "She says, Miss Celie, I adore you." Then she pulls away and kisses me on the lips.

The regal elite of the Mughals indulged in both homosexuality and pederasty, the latter known as "pure love" and popular among Central Asians. In India, however, this was not as widespread. Burhanpur's governor was slain by a young attendant with whom he tried sexual relations. Ali Quli Khan was seen having homosexual encounters with males. According to Sarmad Kashani's history, which was written by the shrine's guardians, he fell in love with a Hindu kid named Abhai Chand, whose father ultimately relented and let them to live together. In late mediaeval Urdu poetry, the term "chapti" was used to refer to intercourse between persons of the same gender. Those who preferred young men were referred to as "Amarad Parasts."Johan Stavorinus, a Dutch explorer, noticed male homosexuality among Mughals in Bengal. "The Sodom sin is not only prevalent in practice among them, but it also extends to bestial relationship with brutes, notably sheep. Women have gone so far as to perpetrate heinous crimes. "The Fatawa-e-Alamgiri of the Mughal Empire defined a uniform set of punishments for homosexuality, including 50 lashes for a slave, 100 lashes for a free infidel, and death by stoning for a Muslim. Kari's main character is a lesbian lady. Amruta Patil, a talented graphic novelist, developed it as a piece of art. Kari, on the other hand, is much more than a lesbian graphic book. It's a viewpoint on the kind of culture we live in. It shows the reader how society presupposes certain things and seeks to shape us as human beings. It's a profoundly gripping story about the struggle to find one's own identity in an increasingly prominent culture riven by variety and injustice. In Lihaaf, the lesbian identity, the Muslim home, and the patriarchal society are all reinvented. The Nawab and his wife's relationship's nonreproductive assumption serves as the foundation for the unfolding of gay pleasure in a dysfunctional Muslim family.

To summarize, homosexuality in various forms exists and will continue to exist. People have battled for the rights of LGBTQ people in the past and will continue to fight in the future. Similarly, the law will continue to evolve, sometimes in favour and sometimes against. It is us who need to change the mentality and accept the people the way they are.

Note: Please look for the references and given and references given inside.

References:

> *Terminology of homosexuality:*
> https://www.hrw.org/news/2019/06/24/section-377-history-young-lgbt-indians-need-concrete-policies-protect-them-bullying
> *https://en.wikipedia.org/wiki/Homosexuality_in_India,* History of Lesbian, Gay, Bisexual and Transgender Social Movements
> Bonnie J. Morris, PhD, George Washington University, Washington, D.C.-"Whey ting be Dat?" The Treatment of Homosexuality in African Literature

Additional works cited:

> Alison Bechdel, Fun Home: A Family Tragicomic, Houghton Mifflin, 2006
> Kate Bornstein, Gender Outlaws: On Men, Women, and the Rest of Us, Routledge, 1994
> Michael Bronski, A Queer History of the United States, Beacon Press, 2011

➢ Devon Carbado and Dwight McBride, eds. Black Like Us: A Century of Lesbian, Gay and Bisexual African-American Fiction, Cleis Press, 2002

➢ David Carter, Stonewall: The Riots That Sparked the Gay Revolution, Macmillan, 2004

➢ Debbie Cenziper and Jim Obergefell, Love Wins: The Lovers and Lawyers Who Fought the Landmark Case for Marriage Equality, Harper Collins Publishers, 2016

➢ Lillian Faderman, The Gay Revolution: The Story of the Struggle, Simon & Schuster, 2015; and To Believe in Women: What Lesbians Have Done for America – A History, Houghton Mifflin, 1999

➢ Leslie Feinberg, Transgender Warriors, Beacon Press, 1996

➢ Sue-Ellen Jacobs, Two-Spirit People: Native American Gender Identity, Sexuality and Spirituality, University of Illinois, 1997

➢ David Johnson, The Lavender Scare: The Cold War Persecution of Gays and Lesbians in the Federal Government, University of Chicago Press Books, 2004

➢ Cherrie Moraga and Gloria Anzaldua, This Bridge Called My Back: Writings by Radical Women of Color, Persephone Press, 1981

➢ Daphne Scholinski, The Last Time I Wore a Dress, Riverhead Books 1998

➢ Randy Shilts, And the Band Played On: Politics, People, and the AIDS Epidemic, St. Martin's Press, 1987

➢ Donn Short, Don't Be So Gay! Queers, Bullying, and Making Schools Safe, UBC Press, 2013

➢ Ryan Thoreson, Transnational LGBT Activism, University of Minnesota Press, 2014

➢ Urvashi Vaid, Virtual Equality, Anchor Books, 1995

CHAPTER-10

Transgenderism: A Psycho-Social Facet of Dysphoria

- S. Mariena Kamala Brinda Noel

marienanb1225@gmail.com

Introduction:

The very concept of Transgenders or Hijras in our country is not new. In History, they were given importance and they played a vital role in the King's chamber. But as days passed, the importance deteriorated generation after generation, and today, they do not even have a place to live. Their survival has become a question mark. They undergo so much mental stress and insults throughout their lives.

What does this term Dysphoria mean? They have a struggle in their belongingness. They are not given importance as we think. The world portrays them very sophisticatedly, but the truth lies behind them. They undergo so much stress and depression not knowing where they belong to when they find their real self.

To fit into society and find a place of hope has become a difficult task for many of the Transgenders. Where will they be buried after death? Who will take care of them? None in society is bothered. We see so many of them on streets begging and many into prostitution, what is the reason. Why will they be there if they are given a place in society?

We talk about gender roles, worry about the gender gap, and talk about one's sexual behavior. To talk about sexuality, we can talk about the French Hermaphrodite named Herculine Barbin whose memoirs Foucault published. In mythology, Hermaphroditus the son of Hermes and Aphrodite merged with his lover to become a being with female breasts and male genitals. But she prays to God that the two be united. Imagine the importance given to the person as a human being and the identity. In the past, the human body was only a matter of degree rather than kind.

Causes of Transgenderism

Scientific evidence has shown that certain brain structures in the hypothalamus (the BSTc region) determine each person's core gender feelings and innate gender identity. These structures are "hard-wired" prenatally in the lower brain centers and central nervous system (CNS) during the early stages of pregnancy. If something goes amiss in the early stages of pregnancy the sex hormones do not have the usual action on the integration of the foetus' s brain. In these cases, children are born having a brain-sex (neurological sex) and innate gender identity opposite to that indicated both by their genes and their genitalia.

Being raised in the wrong gender causes them profound gender dysphoria and mental anguish as they grow up. People believed that transgenderism was a lifestyle choice and this belief led to the social stigma attached to the term. Some of the psychological factors which have been linked with transgenderism are parental rejection, absence of a father during childhood, having an emotionally distant father, peer pressure, perfectionism, media images, self-rejection, and poor self-esteem which may be reinforced by hostile reception from society.

Gender transition is the period where the person begins changing their appearance to match their bodies with their internal identity. During the transition, they are very vulnerable to discrimination and are in dire need of support from family and friends. They are often rejected, neglected, or abused by their guardians and choose a life on the streets rather than remain in hostile environments.

This may be a time of excitement and struggle as the person seeks to develop a sense of true self while balancing feelings of guilt and shame, pressures to conform, and the need for secrecy. Individuals may adopt social modifications such as using cross-gender pronouns or gender-neutral names.

All transgenders suffer from great psychological and emotional pain due to the conflict between their gender identity and their original gender role. They find their only recourse is to change their gender role and undergo gender reassignment therapy. Often a minimum time of psychological counseling is required, and a minimum time spent living in the desired gender role to ensure they can function psychologically in that role. They need to be prepared for everything after the surgery as they will be facing a different world.

Psychosocial Problems of Transgenders

There is an interrelation between our thinking, feeling, and behavior or the psychological realm which includes family, society culture, and norms. This interrelation is called psychosocial. If society accepts one's behavior, one can adjust to society. If not, one cannot find a balance between one's needs and society's expectations. This imbalance can have an impact on an individual's thinking, emotions, and behavior and can lead to psychosocial problems (anxiety, low self-esteem, guilt, etc.) which can affect wellbeing and quality of life. Psychological symptoms are the manifestations of psychosocial problems. A lifetime of this can be very challenging and can sometimes cause anxiety disorders, depression, and other mental illnesses. The most common mental health issues transgender persons experience is depression as well as adjustment, anxiety, personality, and post-traumatic stress disorders.

Choosing to be openly gender variant in the transition process for a transsexual can result in the loss of family and friends who disapprove or do not understand. The loss can be particularly traumatic if, as is often the case, the disclosure or discovery of the person's transgender status is unplanned. "In many circumstances, being forced or even choosing to disclose without being fully prepared for what disclosure involves can have devastating consequences." (Israel and Tarver, 1997). There is some evidence that transgendered persons may be less likely to seek treatment for depression, fearing that their gender issues will be assumed to be the cause of their symptoms and that they will be judged negatively. Parental rejection leads to low self-esteem and a negative self-image (Bolin, 1988). Transgender youth are marginalized both in mainstream society and in lesbian, gay, bisexual (LGB) compounding their risk.

They experience some form of victimization as a direct result of their transgender identity or presentation. This victimization ranges from subtle forms of harassment and discrimination to blatant verbal, physical, and sexual assault, including beatings, rape, and even homicide. Many assaults against transgender persons are never reported to the police. Hijras provide several reasons justifying their alcohol consumption that range from the need to 'forget worries' and to manage rough clients in their sex work life.

Quality of Life is the subjective judgment of the extent to which one is living the good life. This perception of the good life may be based on feelings of happiness, meaning in life, and inner peace. The definition of quality of life is different for everyone. The main thing that determines the quality of life is our ability to enjoy all that life has to offer. Quality of life (QOL) defined as a person's perception of his or her physical and mental health (Wong, Cronin, Griffith, Irvine, & Guyatt, 2001), covers broad domains including physical, psychological, economical, spiritual, and social well-being. QOL is described by the World Health Organization (WHO) as "people's perception of their situation in the culture and the value system they live in related with their goals, standards, expectations and ideas" (Alleyne, 2003). It is a broad-ranging concept affected in a complex way by the person's physical health, psychological state, personal beliefs, social relationships, and their relationship to salient features of their environment. The term QOL is used to evaluate the general well-being of individuals and societies.

In studies, it has been found that QOL is negatively correlated with levels of anxiety, major depression, and psychological distress in psychiatric inpatients, university counseling center outpatients, and nonclinical undergraduate populations (Frisch, 1994). Because anxious personality is characterized by joylessness, negativity, and dissatisfaction with life (Millon, 1996) it can be expected that anxious personality should correlate negatively with the overall level of self-reported QOL. Outside of basic health care needs, the goal of medical therapy for transgender people is to improve their quality of life by facilitating a transition to a physical state that more closely represents their sense of themselves.

Self Esteem reflects a person's overall self-appraisal of one's worth. Self-esteem encompasses both beliefs and emotions. Psychologists usually regard self-esteem as an enduring personality characteristic (trait self-esteem), though normal short-term variations (state self-esteem) occur. Self-esteem can apply specifically to a particular dimension or have a global extent. Branden (1969) defined self-esteem as "... the experience of being competent to cope with the basic challenges of life and being worthy of happiness". This two-factor approach, as some have also called it, provides a balanced definition that seems to be capable of dealing with limits of defining self-esteem primarily in terms of competence or worth alone.

Maslow (1954) states that no psychological health is possible unless the essential core of the person is fundamentally accepted loved and respected by others and by himself. Self-esteem allows people to face life with more confidence, benevolence, and optimism, and thus easily reach their goals and self-actualize There is accumulating evidence that positive self-esteem can be an antidote to depression. Self-esteem serves as a buffer from the onslaught of anxiety, guilt, depression, shame, criticism, and other internal attacks.

Harter (1993) said that people's judgment about themselves is an important factor of self-esteem. An important basis for self-judgment is how well one 'stacks up against a reference group. The concept of social comparison has implications in understanding differences in the self-esteem of members in groups that are discriminated such as the gender variant groups. A transgender perceives his or her gender identity to be incongruous with the apparent anatomical reality and this results in boundary stress between core gender identity and physical characteristics. Gender variant children are much more likely to run away from home and even attempt suicide than their heterosexual peers, probably as a form of escape from a dysfunctional family system that resists the notion of a child with a nonconforming identity.

The sting of emotional abuse carries the same effect on self-esteem as physical or sexual abuse. Transgender has its own built-in Catch 22. (Peters, 2005) since one needs very high self-esteem to successfully deal with being transgendered, but simply being transgendered is one of the great forces sapping self-esteem. Peer victimization is a social risk factor for internal distress. People with a diagnosis of social anxiety disorder find social situations nerve-wracking, from mixing with friends to speaking in public. Several explanations have been proposed for why they feel this way, including that they are preoccupied with creating the right impression.

Research has indicated the role of 'core' or 'unconditional' negative beliefs (e.g. I am inept) and 'conditional' beliefs (e.g. If I show myself, I will be rejected) in social anxiety. Some of the negative core beliefs among transgenders are as follows • I'm fundamentally different, and don't fit in. • I'm not worthwhile unless I'm accepted by those I admire. • I can't be accepted by others unless I meet their expectations. • If someone got to know the real me, they wouldn't accept me. • If I draw attention to myself, others will see something they won't like•To be accepted by those I admire, I must compensate for my deficiencies by excelling in some way. • I'm not good enough to be accepted by the people I admire. These are among the common core beliefs that generate problems like social anxiety, depression, and self-esteem.

Young people who sense they may be lesbian, gay, bisexual, or transgender (LGBT) are especially vulnerable to this dynamic of social unacceptability resulting in negative core beliefs. They are often being told that they are sick, sinful, disgusting, and should not exist. Many who cannot hide their differences become the target of violence. Transgenders face the dilemma of being labeled everywhere they go.

They are continuously conscious of the way they appear towards the public and hope that the public will perceive them for the gender they want to be, without repercussions. Studies in animals and humans show that psychological abuse can have long-lasting consequences. People who are bullied constantly are under a lot of stress, and if the situation is not taken care of at the proper time, the victims might suffer from social anxiety and depression.

Down the ages, our society has condemned and alienated people who do not conform to its norms. Transgender persons are one such group of people who have been marginalized in many societies. Leading a life as a transgender is far from easy because such people can be neither categorized as male nor as female and this deviation is "unacceptable" to society's vast majority. Trying to eke out a dignified living is even worse. Research shows that transgenders are even overlooked by the rest of the LGBT community. Transgenders still float beneath the surface, most of them are invisible, like the unseen portion of the iceberg. One of the important problems transgenders face in society is a lack of social acceptance.

Although they have been part of every culture and society in recorded human history, they have only recently become the focus of attention in psychological, medical, and social research. Unchecked negative attitudes toward transgender persons may result in transphobia as well as discriminatory treatment of transgender individuals (Claman, 2008). As The (2002) puts it, ignorance is one of the reasons why people are prejudiced against transsexuals. As the visibility of transgender's increases, it is time to help them join the mainstream of society.

To achieve this objective, it is necessary to understand the psychological issues and challenges they face as well as examine the prevailing attitudes in society. A major challenge in the mobilization process has been motivating transgenders to actively demand rights and services. There have been some progressive steps taken to improve their quality of life, but this has come after years of crushing social stigmatization, abuse, and general derision from the wider community. As one transgender put it "They make documentaries about us and say all these interesting things, but when we walk out on the street, we still get the calling and the whistles." Discrimination is the antithesis of equality, and all right-minded citizens must drive away discriminatory practices from all walks of life.

Conclusion:

Transgenders are also human beings. It's a change that has happened to them that has to be accepted. Accept them as they are. A change must happen first in the minds of their parents then the society. Just because we are blessed, we cannot tease them, give them the space they need and make their lives also happy and make them also feel that there is a purpose for what they are

Works Cited

➢ Arnold H. Grossman (2006). *Transgender youth as a vulnerable population: Findings of a qualitative study.* The Haworth Press, Inc. doi:10.1300/J082v51n01_06 facial feminization surgery or gender reassignment surgery. Qual Life Res. 2010 Sep;19(7):1019-24. Epub 2010 May 12.

➢ Bilodeau, B. (2003, October 23). *Genderqueer: Understanding transgender student identities.* Paper presented at the AERA Research on Women in Education Annual Conference, Knoxville, TN.

➢ Branden, N. (1969). *The psychology of self-esteem.* New York: Bantam.

CHAPTER-11

Queer Theory: A Study on The Structure of The Autobiographical Texts

-Anamika Saha

anamikasaha1292@gmail.com

Many works have been written on homosexuality and is experiencing ongoing evolution, be it fiction, non-fiction or critical writings. There are many prominent writers and activists like Smt. L. N. Tripathi, who are representing queer community of South Asia to the world. But there is something that most of us are missing in the process of awareness: **exotification, elevation** and **acceptance**. It is an undeniable fact that we destroy what we elevate; hence it is time to elevate things cautiously or, if possible, not to elevate at all. And this precisely is the point where we go too far from the agenda of acceptance.

A.Revathi's *The Truth About Me: A Hijra Life Story* clearly presents the truth of the attempts to be 'visible' to the society, especially practices like when they clap or their style of singing and dancing did not and could not remain just an occupation. These acts become a fundamental part of their identity; the identity no human would desire to own but gifted by the society to them. It is not only limited to the Hijras, but all those who are heterosexual or 'biologically unfit' as the misogynists call it. With flashy make ups or dresses, it is an attempt, consciously or subconsciously, to be seen. Of course, there is nothing right or wrong about that; every human being carries the urge to be recognized and to be accepted. The attempts to be seen mostly seem a failure; rather it becomes an act of revolution and vigilance against the structure to its existence. And to understand this critically, it is necessary to trace all the experiences of the people who identify themselves within and outside the structure.

Most of the texts begin with the biological anatomy and the void it creates within the person dealing with the sexual identity crisis. As Smt. L.N. Tripathi shares in her book *Red Lipstick: The Men in My Life*:

"When I was born, the doctor checked my genitals and pronounced me a boy. Who could foretell that a claim like that, a seemingly innocuous gesture, would make me for life? What we are assigned as at birth – male or female is our gender. And somewhere along the way, we human beings decided that the gender would dictate our lives, steer us down certain paths, brand our behaviour and inform almost all our choices..." (1, *Red Lipstick: The Men in my Life*)

This perplexity that most of the people who identify themselves as 'different' is worth considering. The position of '**not understanding**' or the '**gap**' itself is given - given by the phallagocentric structure. The problem begins by not understanding the social functions based on **biology**, leading to the confusion of the multiple roles an individual play within the society to sustain as our society is clearly limited to the division of roles based on mere genitals, that is, that can be seen and consequently ready to gulp. In all those autobiographies that represent the queer community, the declaration of the confusion as an issue accelerates the acceptance of heterogeneity from the society that seeks homogeneity. One cannot ignore the fact that the existence of the gap between the sign system could be understood at a very early age:

	Signifier	**Signified**
NORMAL parts	Man ———————	Penis/phallus
	Woman —————	Vulva/lady

	Signifier	**Signified**
'AB'NORMAL	Man————————	Vulva/lady parts
	Woman—————————	Penis/phallus

As we can see when a human identifies itself with his vulva/phallus, the structure is at the state of status quo. But when the person identifies itself with the other genital or does not identify itself at all, it questions the binary which is the fundamental foundation of the structure to sustain. If we perceive the art forms like the movie *The Danish Girl* directed by Tom Hooper, the gap is clearly presented. The urge to be accepted and the feeling of being the way one identifies itself are binaries and consequently, juxtaposed crushing the constructive idea of the given identity. When the possibility of the other possibilities stirs the status quo of the prevailing structure, unrest is inevitable beginning the chronology of **alienation, exotification** and **appropriation**.

The texts that represent the queer studies narrate their struggle for their identity and power and if considered carefully, we find stages common to the texts. The first stage belongs to the 'Given' and 'Desired' and the speaker is crushed between the two. With many instances to communicate with the heterogeneous structure, they establish the presence of something that has been existing since the beginning. This is where the argument of nature/culture begins. Not recognizing with the functioning of the genitals provided by nature is not natural and yet it is as the confusion that rises is natural and cultural at the same time.

The second stage is when they have identified themselves but acceptance is the issue. In this stage the complication accelerates weaved with the sexual orientation; here the perplexity of identity develops to a whole new 'cultural identity'. Claude Levi Strauss called it 'scandal' but this is not all. This new identity provides acceptance to the self and the active realization of its own voice leading to third stage and hence, we can call it a transformation stage.

The third stage is cultural; the struggle to be seen and to bring 'changes' within the structure creating mayhem. This change brings the power – power of 'being' and to disrupt the structure 'actively' with deliberate movements of fission and fusion. And with this disruption they establish their identity within the society; the same society that once denied their existence. The entire experience has been voiced for the world to listen and acknowledge their presence within the structure. This is not mere cultural as they have been 'accused' most of the times; it is natural and culture is a part of that 'natural'. Consequently, it would not be wrong to state that the 'queer theory' cannot be limited within single coffer.

Coming back to **exotification**, there are two ways to perceive the function and mechanism of its nature. Exotification can either elevate or demean one's presence; in either case it is harmful. The queer group, specifically the Hijra community experiences both the mechanisms. When they visit anyone's house on the occasion of child birth or marriage to bless, they are being elevated as the Messiah and the people seek blessings from the representatives of the community. On the other hand, this exotification causes the harassment, prostitution and much other exploitation which is unbearable for any human being. In fact, *badhaii* and prostitution are the fundamental occupations for the community to earn. Gradually the scenario is changing with the interference of the government to uplift the community.

Yet, the lack of acceptance is evident culturally among the common people. To uproot this exotification is vital for the acceptance. But this is not possible until the recognition and acceptance blend in – not by elevation/demotion but by considering them as human beings by bringing a revolution into our day to day discourse. Because if we try to erase exotification in the stage when nothing is developed the entire process of struggle 'to be seen' would perish. Their '**differences**' is their identity; or we should say their '**differences**' that has been categorised by the phallogocentric system has created and established their identity today.

To provide this identity a concrete plinth in the present it is necessary to establish a cultural history. As a result, we will find many texts narrating histories from the myths or politics. References from the texts like Kamasutra, Mahabharata or Ramayana advocate the contribution of the community providing assurance not only to their existence but also the benefaction as association to prevailing society. To trace the political contribution, the Hijra community has always contributed from the pre-Mughal period to the British. In the journal *'Historical Evolution of Transgender Community in India'* by M.Michetray, he has presented the history as well as short introduction to the criminalization of the community.

"In the second half of the 19th century, the British colonial administration vigorously sought to criminalize the hijra community and to deny them the civil rights. Hijras were considered to be separate caste or tribe in different parts of India by the colonial administration. The criminal tribes Act, 1871, this included all hijra who were considered in kidnapping and castrating children and dressed like women to dance in public places." (18)

Such criminalization by the 'dominants' has injected the venom within the society to such an extent that the effect can be felt even today. The entire process of targeting a particular 'community' is political; the power structure we see is unblemished. The British had strategically earmarked a particular set of people to criminalize them. They had criminalized every possible community irrespective of religion, gender or class/caste whoever stood against them. But those communities were gloriously titled as national defenders or fighters. But the stain on the transgender community still exists among commons and this happens not due to the lack of knowledge of their existence but the misinformation and the crippled medium of awareness that failed to accelerate even the basic interest to inculcate their *existence*. Moreover, this age-old falsified criminalization has become a fundamental myth today on which the entire structure of denial exists.

In general, the structure exotifies what it does not understand as it is been inculcated within all of us during the process of upbringing that everything around us exists is with a binary, that is, relational. In fact, Ferdinand de Saussure, the Swiss linguist, presented his theory of binary that clearly acknowledges the practice of identity based on binary. It was this theory that has bluntly presented the fundamental flaw of our structure. Though the French anthropologist Claude Levi-Strauss had highlighted the existence of the elements between the binary and entitled it as the *scandal,* the attempt lacks the effect on the 'generals' within the structure. Jacques Derrida, too, took Strauss as the prominent figure to the discourse of the *scandal* yet it was nearly impossible to uproot the age-old belief in a single blow. What Saussure had presented in his theory was something that already existed within the 'mainstream' culture making it easier to inculcate the already-accepted ideologies and practices. On the other hand, what Strauss and Derrida did was broader than the former hypothesis. It was not limited to the **acceptables**; it went beyond where no discourse could reach before them. And hence, the discourse cripples even today when we attempt to understand the *scandal* using the language of binary.

Acknowledgement is easy; in the current scenario everyone 'knows' about the existence of the queer. But if we maintain a regular discourse with the people, a few would be clear about the queer community as well as the differences between the concepts of gender, sex and sexuality. Unfortunately, most of the people possess either the manipulated and falsified knowledge or no knowledge at all, resulting in hostile attitude towards them and psychological effects on the heterosexual demography like homophobia. Due to lack of proper knowledge, the people create speculations among themselves, fuelled by the fake information regarding criminalization by the British Raj, forgetting the untold contribution of the Hijra community before and during the imperial period.

The major cause for the existence of such a black hole is the selection of historical knowledge and linguistic haemorrhage. Most of the historical texts do not narrate the contribution of the community, or even their existence. While scrutinizing the historical records, one would clearly notice the domination of phallagocentrism; the achievements, sacrifices and failures of men. Even the women were few; even they have been carefully selected to glorify and elevate for the sake of presenting the society in a particular hue. There is a huge gap between told/untold histories; the *untolds* are dumped into the black hole, never to be revived. In such practices, many groups and communities become anonymous resulting in becoming victims of what we call **identity assassination**. The queer community is one of them.

Many attempts are being made by the scholars of various fields to re-establish and reassert the long lost position of the queer community on the basis of both intellectual and cultural aspects of their identity. Books like *Shikhandi: And Other Tales They Don't Tell You* by the renowned mythologist Devdutt Pattanaik, *Because I Have a Voice: Queer Politics in India* by Gautam Bhan, *Queer Activism in India: A Story in the Anthropology of Ethics* by Naisargi N. Dave and many others are contributing to the firm establishment of the foundation of queer community not based on something mere fresh but foregrounding and idealizing the '**untold historical silhouette.**'

But unfortunately, this is not enough. Another aspect to be noted is the language that we use in our regular chores. As mentioned before, the structure of our language is crippled; it demands reinvention. Language is the ground on which any abstract transforms itself to evidence. Currently, the language is distorted; it is not adequate to understand something through the medium exclusively based on binary. Elaine Showalter, focussing towards *gynocriticism*, that is, writings about women by women in the language favourable to women, in 1981, highlighted a vital factor to bring revolution of acceptance and recognition. She stated Nelly Furman in her Feminist Criticism in the Wilderness that,

"'It is through the medium of language that we define and categorize areas of difference and similarity, which in turn allow us to comprehend the world around us. Male-centred categorizations predominate in American English and subtly shape our understanding and perception of reality; this is why attention is increasingly directed to the inherently oppressive aspects for women of a male-constructed language system." (316)

This politics is not merely limited to a single geographical area; the phenomenon is widespread to every country and their respective discourses. The gaps the prevailing language carries create a mayhem affecting the entire *play* within the structure. Just like '*gynocriticism*' for women, the queer must possess a language of their own to provide a path towards a smooth politics of understanding and recognition, not validation.

The politics of existence in a society promoting complexity under the veil of simple structure, hence, demands more than merely 'seen'. To be seen is not a solution; what is seen can be unseen easily. And this is happening since ages. It is not possible as a structure to erase the boundary completely but it is definitely possible to push it a little further as change is nature. And if one argues on the nature, one must not forget the cosmos as we know till today is expanding its boundary with each passing moment towards the infinity; the infinity is beyond our intellect. And so, we need not question nature when we are a 'part' of it.

References

1. Butler, Judith. *Gender Trouble*. n.p.: n.d.
2. Derrida, Jacques. *Structure, Sign and Play in the Discourse of Human Sciences*. n.p. n.d.
3. Laxmi, Pooja Pande. *Red Lipstick: The Men in My Life*. Penguin Books. New Delhi, 2016.
4. Michetray,M. *Historical Evolution of Transgender Community in India*. Review of Social Sciences. vol. 4. no.1. 2015. pp.17-19.
5. Pattanaik, Devdutt. *Shikhandi: And Other Tales They Don't Tell You*. Zubaan ,Penguin Books. New Delhi, 2014.
6. Revathi,A. *The Truth About Me: A Hijra Life Story*. Translated by V. Geetha. Penguin Books. New Delhi, 2009.

7. Showalter, Elaine. *Feminist Criticism in the Wilderness*. n.p. : n.d.

8. Spivak, Gayatri Chakravorty. *"Can The Subaltern Speak?"*. planetarities.web.unc.edu>files>2015/01.pdf

9. *The Danish Girl*, created by Tom Hooper, performed by Eddie Redmayne. Focus Features, Universal Pictures. 2015.

-------------------------------THE END-------------------------------

For contacting publication, VISIT:

Website:- www.sotpublication.com

Instagram:- https://www.instagram.com/spectrum.of.thoughts/

LinkedIn:- https://www.linkedin.com/company/spectrum-of-thoughts

Twitter:- https://twitter.com/spectrumpublish